The
Book
Sisters

Hope Andersen

HOPE ANDERSEN wrote her first novel at the age of 60. In her early career as a writer, she published both short fiction and poetry. She was awarded the Wellesley College Playwriting Award for her one-act play *Room*, which was produced at the Lyric Stage, Boston. She has worked intermittently over the years as a newspaper critic, a ghostwriter, an editor, a teacher, and a screenwriter. A native New Englander, she now lives in North Carolina with her husband Thom. They have three grown children, two dogs, a cat and a fish. She is currently at work on a young adult novel titled *An Accidental Thief*.

WHAT A FRIEND YOU ARE
Words and Music by TOM PAXTON
Copyright © 1972 (Renewed) EMI U CATALOG, INC.
All Rights Controlled by EMI U CATALOG, INC. (Publishing)
and ALFRED PUBLISHING, LLC (Print)
All Rights Reserved
Used by Permission of ALFRED MUSIC

Cover photo by Alexander Shustov (courtesy of Unsplash.com)

for my family
with love

ACKNOWLEDGEMENTS

I am deeply grateful to the following people who supported and encouraged me in so many ways: my husband Thom, without whom none of this would have been possible; my children, Nicholas, Haldis, and Kylie who read, listened, and loved me during it all. I thank you for bearing with me and believing in me.

Thanks to my sisters Ursula, Sarah, and Felicity who blessed me with unconditional support.

Thanks to my friend Carol Prendergast, my *Artists Way* buddy, who dared me to venture into uncharted waters. And to authors Madison Smartt Bell and Hazel Dawkins who provided early encouragement and hope.

Special thanks to all these friends. Without their support, this project might never have come to be: Elizabeth Poreba, Donna Milligan, Carol Houle, Timothy Wise, Frank Gilroy, Meg Smeaton, Steve Strachan, Keith Bayless, Debbie Moss, Debra Harr, Nancy Marshburn, Ginger Equi, Lorna Bishop, Dan Ryan, Connie Burrow and several others who wish to remain anonymous.

To my early editor, Ellen Eller, I give thanks. I know I caught you at a hard time, and you were gracious. To my daughter Haldis, who provided a most thorough second editing job, I am grateful. And to the editors at Book Baby who took a final crack at the manuscript, thank you. I appreciate all that the folks at Book Baby have done for me, especially Sandro Braidotti, who has been the best.

Let me not forget Peggy Williamson who worked so diligently with me on the discussion questions. Her input and insights are greatly appreciated, as is her unswerving belief in my ability.

Finally, I would be remiss if I didn't mention two old friends, long since passed: Tom Cole, who told me years ago that I had this book in me, and George Garrett, who saw my promise when I could not see it myself.

THE BOOK SISTERS

PROLOGUE

Iowa was hot and flat in 1963. The air had been standing still for weeks and inhaling the moisture that was the pond behind the Book's big white farmhouse until little enough of it remained, so little, in fact, that when the dogs took turns trying to lap up the puddles where before the pond had been, they emerged with paws muddied to their knees, dirty noses, and soiled tongues. The cicada, invisible in the thirsty trees, screeched monotonously, sawing feverishly at the thick air with their high-pitched cries. It was hot, so hot that the roads shimmered like lakes, and the knee-high corn, which stretched out in acres from the house, was parched and dry.

Vera Book, the fourth of the six Book sisters, was tired of lying on her bed reading comics as the fan in the girls' room swept back and forth like wings, leaving a wake of cool air that momentarily refreshed and then was gone again. She looked over at Virginia, her younger sister, who lay asleep on her bed, her wavy brown hair spread out around her except where sweat-soaked tendrils lay plastered to her face. At six years old, Virginia was possibly the most beautiful of the Book sisters, although each girl appeared glorious in her own way, as Valley, their mother, would constantly remind them. Next to Virginia's bed rested Viveca's little cot, just the right size now for the four-year-old, but soon to be too small. Viveca slept too, in her little blue shorts and striped T-shirt, the same thing that all the girls wore. The Books believed in hand-me-downs. They couldn't afford not to. Only Victoria Book, the oldest sister, ever got new clothes and that was because she was the oldest and she had to have new clothes for her job. She played the organ every Sunday at the services for the United Methodist Church, and Victoria would rather die than go there looking like a pauper. Valley couldn't help but appease her.

Vera hopped down from her bed and tiptoed out of the room, down the long flight of stairs to the kitchen where Valley sat at the kitchen table shelling peas. The kitchen was quiet except for the hum of the refrigerator and spotless. Though the green countertops and yellow cupboards were nothing new, they shone like a teacher's apple on the first day of school. The red speckled linoleum floor was clean enough to eat off of. Everything sparkled and smelled just fine, like fresh air and peaches.

"Valley," Vera began. "Can I have a lemonade stand?"

Valley looked up from her peas and thought. Valley Book, born Evelyn Forester, was a handsome woman and kind. Everybody loved Valley—her children, her friends from church, her siblings, and her spouse. Especially, her spouse, Vern Book. He had loved her ever since he first laid eyes on her in the stairwell at the recruiting center that sultry afternoon in September 1943. They were both signing up to aid, however they could, in the fight against the German monster, and not just the man but the machine that was an instrument of intolerance and hate. Neither of them had been political before. Like most Americans, they just sailed along enjoying the comforts of democracy and praying that nothing disastrous would happen again in their lives. But here it loomed, Fascism, decked out in red and black with spidery swastikas and rigid salutes, ready to wipe out not only a people but people everywhere who did not conform to the perfect standard by which it ruled.

Valley, a journalist by profession, was assigned to work with the army's records bureau in which she documented the stories of those Americans fighting abroad, capturing their wartime experiences in the prose that only she could deliver. Her stories, which were used to conjure up interest in the wartime effort back home and, hopefully, encourage young Americans to enlist for service while inspiring those unable to serve to keep making sacrifices back home, were accompanied by photos taken by none other than a young man named Vern Book.

Book's photos became even more instrumental in pushing people into the fight than were Evelyn's words. Her words required time and concentration, and thought. But Vern's photos were immediate. One look at the soldier with the severed foot holding a limp child whose life had been blown away by a tommy gun raised immediate ire. And those secret shots taken of prisoners of war wearing ludicrous striped pajamas and ridiculous striped surgeon's caps while being herded in single rows to certain death couldn't help but move even the hardest heart. After the war was over, Vern had offers from *The Baltimore Sun, The Chicago Tribune, The New York Times.* But he was through with the horrors of the world. He decided to buy a farm in Iowa and to look at nothing but animals and corn for the rest of his life. And Valley. He wanted always to see her, every day, every minute of his life.

Valley smiled a bittersweet smile remembering all this and the way that Vern had proposed to her, not with a ring but with a key, a small golden key that she wore around her neck and never took off.

"Will you take this key, the key to my heart, the key to my future, the key to my life, and be with me forever?" he asked as he knelt on one knee before her. They were in Washington, D.C. It was April 1946 and the cherry blossoms were out. As Valley sat on the cold marble bench with the sunlight so bright against the robin's egg blue sky, a little wind set the blossoms falling, showering her like snow, and she just started laughing. Laughing and laughing. Isn't this rich, she thought to herself. Laughing.

Vern started to rise, mistaking her laughter for rejection. But she gently pushed him down with both hands on his shoulders and leaned over close to him and said, "There is nothing, nothing on Earth that would make me happier." Only then did he tell her about the farm.

"Valley," Vera said insistently. "Can I have a lemonade stand? I'm so bored and there's nothing to do. And it's so hot."

"Of course, sweetheart. I'll make the lemonade. You get out the cups and we'll set out of some of the zucchini bread and a few of the vegetables." Valley watched the little girl scamper off to the pantry for napkins, cups, and paper plates, shaking her head and hoping that someone, anyone, would come along and buy a cup, though the likelihood of that seemed very slim as no one ever came this way except the mailman and the neighbors who lived five and ten miles away. Or a stranger who got lost. But if Valley believed anything, she believed in hope. An optimistic outlook, scanning the horizon for possibilities, could assuage many a disappointed effort or a terrible scare. Valley did not consider herself to be a religious woman, but she did subscribe to Possibilitarianism, if such a thing existed. It did, in her mind.

"What are you going to do for a table?" asked Vern, who had come in from the barn for a beverage and caught the tail end of the conversation.

Vera looked at her father and then at her mother and back again at her dad. "I thought maybe just one of the big cardboard boxes your stuff comes in."

"Too flimsy," he said. "I have an idea. Come with me." He chugged his lemonade down and headed back to the barn with Vera following, excited. There Vern took out a couple of sawhorses; together they carried them and set them under the giant elm in the front yard. Next, he found a piece of plywood, left over from when he built the chicken coop. It was discolored and warped slightly, decorated by webs, but Vera was not discouraged. Valley covered its blemishes with a floral cloth. Together they set out the cups and jug, the plates, and the baskets of food. And a little tin box for the money that Vera hoped she would make that afternoon. And so the lemonade stand was created.

Vera settled in under the shade of the great tree and waited for someone to come along. While she waited, she did what Vera always did. She wrote stories. Now she went back to a story that she had written, reread it, and set to fixing it to make it more real. It was titled *Summer Vacation* and was about a girl her age who wanted to make some money over the summer. Only she didn't want to babysit or run a lemonade stand. (The irony of that was not lost on Vera, who had not yet learned the term "irony" but who recognized that the fact that she was running a lemonade stand contradicted what she said in her story.) Anyway, in the story, the character, Roxy, decides instead to set up a funeral home for dead animals. At every funeral, Roxy performs a poem which she has written especially for the occasion.

As Vera looked up from her writing, momentarily sucking on the end of a blue ballpoint pen, she saw something in the distance. A mirage? She wondered. But no, it was a cloud of dust moving toward her down the road. Dust, which could only mean a tornado or a car, and this day, with its infinitely blue, cloudless sky was not a day for tornadoes. She watched the puff grow closer and closer until suddenly it was there, a big car, aqua blue and white, with silver rims and sharp fins, so shiny that she wondered how the dust had not stuck to it. It pulled up next to the stand and stopped. Then, a tall, skinny man in a piercing white suit stepped out of the car, removed the straw hat from his head, and ran his fingers through his thin, blonde hair to get it out of his eyes.

"Cedar Rapids?" he asked succinctly.

Speechless, Vera pointed north. "You can't miss it," she croaked. "There are signs."

Having ascertained his location, he perused the table for refreshments. "What have we here?" he asked, picking up the lemonade jug and tipping it into his throat until the entire contents was gone.

Vera couldn't keep her jaw from dropping. She didn't know whether she should feel affronted or amazed.

"I guess that's about $5 worth," the man said, removing his fat wallet from his pocket and laying down a $5 bill on the table. "How much?" he asked picking up a loaf of zucchini bread.

"Seventy-five cents each," Vera responded quickly.

"I'll take four," he said, laying another $5 bill on the table. Then, he loaded some vegetables in a brown bag and Vera weighed them. More money appeared, and Vera was getting giddy with the cash. This was a windfall! More cash than she had ever taken in on a single day, in a week, maybe even a month! She wished there were more to give to the man who seemed to be in a buying mood.

Then, he looked over at her composition book. "What's this?" he asked curiously, picking up the journal.

"Oh that, that's nothing. Just some stories I'm working on. They're not for sale," Vera said, trying to take the book back, but he held it in a firm grip and high above her head.

"You're a writer?" he asked. Vera nodded. "The reason I ask is I'm always on the lookout for new writers. And books. What's this book called??"

"The Book Sisters."

He laughed. "Really? What's this book about?"

"My family. Kind of. Our last name is Book and there are six of us sisters, plus Valley and Vern."

"Well, I'll be. So, this is kind of a memoir." Vera didn't know what a memoir was, but she didn't feel that she could let this stranger know that.

"Sort of." she replied.

"And what is the purpose of this book?" he asked.

"To share our life," she answered proudly.

The man opened one of the bags of zucchini bread and took a big bite. "Um, delicious," he said. "Say, you wouldn't have some more lemonade, would you?"

Vera was torn. If she left him at the table, he might take all the produce and just leave like that, taking her journal with him.

If she didn't get the lemonade and he was honorable, she'd never hear the end of it from Valley. He must have seen her apprehension, because he took his car keys out of his pocket and handed them to Vera.

"Don't worry. I'm not going anywhere," he said, winking. "The name is Kennett. Kennett Jenkins. You tell your mama I'd like to meet her too." He waved up toward the window where Valley stood in her shapeless yellow dress, looking out. She gave a little wave back and then smoothed her hair, letting the curtain fall. Vera took the lemonade jug and ran up to the house, knowing something good was going to come of this day.

It turned out that Kennett Jenkins was a publisher from New York traveling across country to writers' conferences, scoping new talent, and giving talks. Later, he would tell Vera that when he first saw her book, he had just indulged her in a childhood fantasy, but that later, after reading her stories more closely, he felt that he had found a rare talent. Here was a young person, she was only eight, who not only knew how to write but more importantly, how to observe, listen, and think.

"You've got a great idea here," he said, tapping the journal with his long fingers, "but it needs to percolate. Wait another twenty or thirty years and then you'll be ready to write it. But don't rush it. When it comes, it will come like a storm." He encouraged Vera to keep working on stories, and to send them to him, and he would try to place them in magazines like *Kids* and *Mirabelle*. "Let's see if we can't make you a published author," he said as he slipped the copy of *Summer Vacation* in his pocket. "But you've got to get older. You're not ready to write that yet. Give it time," he told her again. And then with a tip of his hat, and a lanky wave, in a puff of dust, he was gone.

Vera watched him disappear down the road, diminishing in size and dust until she could see him no longer. Then, she sat down under an elm tree, her knees pulled up to her chest, her arms hugging tight, and focused on every little detail of the encounter. She pulled out her notebook and, sure enough, *Summer Vacation* was gone. It hadn't been a dream. He had been real. And this, she knew, was the beginning of the rest of her life.

SHOOTING STAR

LEGEND HAS IT THAT WHEN VICTORIA, THE OLDEST OF THE SIX
Book sisters, born in 1949, was only two years old, she picked up
the wooden tong of a xylophone that Valley had just purchased
at the church rummage sale for a nickel, and banged out *Twinkle,
Twinkle, Little Star* as though she had been practicing all her life.
Vern thought it was surely a fluke, but Valley was certain that her
baby was a prodigy. She watched Victoria closely, prodding her with
pots and pans on which to bang, harmonicas, and even a small fid-
dle that a neighbor was tossing aside. When she turned four, one of
the neighbor women, Hattie Brown, offered to teach her piano for
free. For Valley, who now had three babies under the age of four and
another one on the way, this seemed a wonderful way to get Victoria
out of the house, to make her feel special and on her own. Victoria
proved a natural and took to the ivory keys like a duck to water. Her
long, slender fingers caressed the ivories and produced songs, some
that she had heard before, some that she made up in her head, but
always with the same precision and feeling that elicited "oohs" and
"aahs" from those who listened.

She kept on with Mrs. Brown for several years, and when she
turned eight, and her feet just touched the ground as she sat on the

piano bench, she gave a recital for the school talent show. Valley, who was concerned that Victoria might freeze during her performance, couldn't have been prouder as she watched and listened to her daughter belt out some of her favorite show tunes and then end with a little slice of Beethoven's *Moonlight Sonata*. Valley had almost burst when friends and strangers came up to her after the performance and congratulated her on Victoria's success, as if Valley were personally responsible, encouraging her to try to the get the child on to *The Ed Sullivan Show*. Or somewhere.

The following year, their church recruited her when the organist left. Nothing seemed too difficult for Victoria to play, as long as it had keys and pedals. And, in this case, stops and levers too. She looked at the music and it translated down into her fingers and out into the world. She received a small stipend for her efforts, which she begrudgingly put back into the family funds, though she would have preferred to save her earnings so that she could one day go to Oberlin or Juilliard in New York City. All Victoria had now was the farm, five younger siblings making noise and demands, high school, which she hated, and her music, which she loved. She counted herself superior to her simple parents, for whom farm life seemed enough, and her tedious siblings who spent all day around horses and cows and cats and then, the weird one, who was always watching and writing, popping up behind sofas when she was making out with her boyfriend or doing personal things. The two youngest were just pixies. Valley called them "the twins," though they were born eighteen months apart, looked nothing like one another, and were different in so many other ways. But they were the apples of Valley's eyes. The afterglow at the end of a spectacular sunset. Valley spoiled them, indulged them in ways none of the older sisters had known, except Violet. Victoria could not wait to escape the chaos and crassness that was her family. But how?

Then, it came, her golden chance. She was seventeen, and almost totally despairing that her life would ever take a turn for the better, when she was invited to go with her piano teacher, Mrs. Brown, and the music director at church, Ms. Aldridge, to a concert in Cedar Rapids at Cornell College. A world-renowned pianist named Barton Barkley, a student of the great Art Tatum, was performing. Needless to say, Victoria was thrilled.

When they arrived at the college, the two women were eager to get out of the hot sun and into the cooler auditorium, but Victoria wanted to explore. She had never stood on a hill before, never seen the sloped land, the way the roads and grass scooped down. She was standing on the highest point in Iowa and she wanted to savor it. She cupped her hands, forming a makeshift telescope, and looked to the north. She knew that somewhere Canada was there and Chicago with its skyscrapers and vast lake and turmoil. She had studied geography in school and was drawn to the maps and photographs of places far away. She imagined herself in Paris, standing at the top of the Eiffel Tower, looking out over the city of sparkling lights. Or California. She whipped around and looked through the telescope to the west. Palm trees and sparkling ocean. Hippies in flowing skirts and scarves, chanting "Love, Love. Love," and hugging one another all the time. Movie stars in convertibles wearing big sunglasses and drinking champagne. Wealth everywhere. She wondered if she could fit in. Then, she looked east to Boston, the symphony and the universities opening doors to a future she'd like to know. She would have liked to go to Oberlin but her father refused to let her apply and she didn't know how to leave. Standing here on this hill that was Cedar Rapids, she knew now. Just walk away, one step at a time. Fear asked her: "Toward what? Toward who?" Courage answered, "you will know."

Victoria's fingers tingled like she wanted to write a song. Even the air felt cooler up here. And for a moment she wished she'd brought a shawl. *Maybe if I move*, she told herself, *I'll warm up*. She only had twenty minutes and no watch, so not wanting to miss the concert, she moved toward the building. And that's when she heard it, the sprinkling and tinkling of notes, trills up and down, and deep bass throbs. They were coming from the open window at the side of the building, so she went over to look. It took a moment for her eyes to adjust.

Through the window, she saw a small room with a piano and a bench and a small metal chair over in the corner. The room was dimly lit and the man at the piano was dark, very black, but she could see his long, dark fingers moving up and down the white keys. Coaxing them to produce the marvelous melodies he was playing. She stood at the window for what felt like the longest time, not wanting to breathe, just savoring every moment, every note. When he finally stopped, resting his fingers in a fan on the keyboard, she exhaled.

Without even looking up, he addressed her, saying, "You can come in you know."

Entering the small room was like entering a cave. Victoria feared he would hear the wild thumping of her heart as she crossed to the chair in the corner, but he just ignored her, continuing to play. It was warm and cozy inside, and the music gave off the heat of a fire. He played and played for a good fifteen minutes, and she sat in awe of his expertise until he finally stopped with a flourish and said, "Time to give a concert."

"You're Art Tatum?" she exclaimed, surprised because she thought Art Tatum was an old man and the man standing in front of her couldn't have been more than 25.

"Hell, no! Art's been dead eight years. I studied with him though. I'm Barton Barkley. Nice to meet you." He held out his hand and she held out hers, although she had never shaken hands with a Negro before. His hands were surprisingly soft and tender, not, she thought, like her own that tended chickens and dug for potatoes and washed dishes in hard water. She pulled back, ashamed. Still, when she did she felt something coursing through her veins. She looked up into his face and almost swooned as the most beautiful eyes, deep, dark chocolate eyes surrounded by white so brilliant it shone, gazed down on her. And his mouth and smile, a dazzling smile with beautiful white teeth, put goose bumps on her arms. At 25, he was handsome, accomplished, refined, and she worshipped him.

"Victoria Book," she managed to whisper.

"Well, Victoria Book," he smiled, "I dedicate this concert to you."

For the concert, he was playing a mix of classical and pop, show tunes, and ragtime. The latter he played first with an energy and playfulness that had the crowd clapping and stomping, even singing along. But when it came to the Rachmaninoff, everyone was silent. He came back onto the stage after the intermission; the lights were dim and he sat in a bowl of gold rays and began. Victoria was surprised by the presence of a full orchestra. Barton Blakeley had played solo for the first half, dancing and cavorting on the keys as if there was no tomorrow. But now things were serious. And with the first dramatic strikes of the keys, Victoria knew this was an experience she would never forget. The interplay of the piano with the rest of the orchestra amazed her; Barton's manipulation of his instrument left her stunned. He sounded like mice running, then cherry petals falling, and then fierce and strenuous like a stallion rearing and bucking. He put his whole body into the music, from the tips of his toes to the tops of his hair, everything was engaged. Then calm again, and smooth. Victoria stood at the silence and started clapping, then noticed she, alone, applauded.

"It's the end of the first movement, dear," Mrs. Brown whispered to her. "No clapping yet. Though he's very good, don't you think?"

Mortified, for the second time that night, she sat down. She had a lot to learn about music, she knew. She also knew that she wanted to learn about it from him. For the rest of the evening, she brooded on how she could see him again, how she could tell him that she must see him again. The impulse was so strong in her, the desire, that she felt her heart racing and her muscles clenching as the need to be with Barton Barkley coursed through her body. She felt tears begin to flow down her cheeks at the thought of never seeing him again, tears which she quickly wiped away when Mrs. Brown asked her, "Are you alright dear?" at which she nodded and took the offered handkerchief and blew her nose. Then, Mrs. Brown patted Victoria's hand in a knowing way, but really, she knew nothing. Yes, the music was beautiful and stirring enough to make you weep, but she wept because she loved him. He was her only hope, and she feared that she would lose him. As he stood and took a bow, Victoria stood too, wanting to sail out of her seat and throw herself in his arms. Instead, she just clapped and wept some more.

Mrs. Brown, reading her mind, or so she thought, suggested that Victoria go and shake hands with Mr. Barkley, thank him for the lovely concert and ask for words of advice. Victoria wavered. She wanted to see him, but not in a crowd, so she told the women she was going to the restroom and then wound her way down the hall toward the little practice space where she had first met him, praying as only a nonbeliever in dire straits can and will pray, "God help me. Bring him to me. I need to see him." And there he was, walking down the hallway, alone, jacket slung over his shoulder.

"Well, hello, Victoria Book," he said, grinning his dazzling white smile.

"You were … you are amazing," she stammered.

He stood in front of her and stroked her cheeks with his soft fingers. "You've been crying."

"I thought I'd never see you again," she said, welling up again.

"Hell, we just met two hours ago!" he laughed, and she joined him.

"I know. And I'm not usually like this. But, I think …"

He put his fingers over her lips. "Don't say it. Here's my card. Tell me a little about yourself." Then, she reached up and pressed her lips on his.

"I love you, Barton Barkley. You be sure I'll be in touch." Then, she ran off back to the women who were standing up on the hill looking at the stars.

"Everything ok?" Mrs. Brown asked.

"Perfect," Victoria smiled as she pressed his card in the palm of her hand where it burned like a bright fire forging a future she had hitherto only imagined, wishing on a star that shot like a whisper across the night sky.

CHANGING TIMES

"Ronnie, Ronnie. It's time." Vern said as he gently shook the sleeping child's shoulder and shone the flashlight into the young girl's face. Veronica, thirteen years old and the second of Vern's six daughters, born in 1951, showed no signs of waking, just a mumbled grunt as she turned over on her side, clutching her pillow closer. Vern turned to leave, saying, "Well, then, I'll do it myself." At that point Ronnie sprung awake as if doused by cold water, eyes open wide, pulling on her red sneakers and tying them at once while imploring her father not to leave without her.

"Quiet down," he said. "You'll wake your sisters," as he flashed the beam of light toward the open bedroom door and out into the hallway and down the long flight of stairs that would lead them out of the house, across the wet grass to the barn. Then, they were immersed in the cool night that was studded with stars, the Milky Way smeared across its face.

Her father had already lit a dim light next to Sapphire's stall, and the beautiful roan mare stood in the straw, her belly protruding, whinnying periodically, and lifting her tail high. Ronnie saw the white bubble emerge with what seemed to be one tiny hoof.

"Has her water broken yet?" Ronnie asked, fully awake now.

"Not yet," Vern replied. "It won't be long now. You coach her through it. Sapphire's your mare. This should be your birth."

Ronnie had no doubts that she could do this. She'd stood next to her father a thousand times as he birthed foals, calves, lambs, puppies, and kittens into this world. She knew enough to give the mare space and to speak softly, to watch for any troubles, but above all, to be patient. Labor could take a while and she knew that. Just like how she knew that when Sapphire's water broke in a gush and she fell to the floor with a plop, it was time. Ronnie entered the stall with her mare and prepared herself to help pull the baby out.

As she watched Sapphire toss and turn in the straw, heaving with each contraction, her legs extended straight and sweeping the straw as if making angels, Ronnie marveled at the miracle of birth. Sticking out now between the two protruding hooves was a face, the sweetest little face. What minutes before had been totally protected in the womb was now emerging into the world, about to begin a life. Sapphire contracted with a groan and Ronnie pulled on the two little legs, and out came the baby with a jiggly burp in a white balloon which Ronnie peeled off deftly revealing a sweet little foal, black with a white exclamation mark on its nose.

"You did good, Sapphire," Ronnie said, stroking the mare. "See your baby? He's a blessing." And that became his name. Blessing Book.

෮ග

Something about that night in the barn really got to Ronnie. It wasn't just the praise her father heaped on her or even the eventual birth of the colt. It was something deeper, the way Sapphire trusted her and listened. The way she, Ronnie, responded to the mare's moves. The way that God packaged small creatures in large creatures and made us all go through this rough ordeal to earn our place on this planet, in this life. Ronnie, who had spent hours with the mother and her colt, was ready for sleep, so just before sunrise, when the roosters were already at it chanting their morning song, Ronnie crawled into her bed. But not before kneeling at her bedside.

Vera, who was always watching everything, thought that Ronnie might be praying. But then, her sister reached under her mattress and took out a notebook and pen. She sat on her bed and started writing. Vera was confused. She was the writer in the family. What could Ronnie possibly be doing? Ronnie looked up as though she could hear Vera's thoughts, so the younger child quickly closed her eyes and pretended she was asleep. But all the while she was plotting how she would find out what Ronnie was up to.

Her father had long hoped that Ronnie would be the one to take over the farm when he was ready to retire. She had all the know-how. She birthed animals and tended the livestock. Year after year, her animals brought blue ribbons and championships from the county fair. She wasn't just good with the farm animals. Lately, she had taken an interest in bees. She had acquired three new hives and she hoped to sell honey soon. Vern knew nothing about that, but he marveled at Ronnie's tenacity and interest. She was no stranger to crops either. While Violet was the mistress of the garden, keeping the family in fruits and vegetables for the winter, Ronnie was there with Vern, plowing, tilling, and planting the acres of corn; and then watching, harvesting, and getting a fair market price.

Farm life just seemed to suit Ronnie, and therefore it was no wonder that Vern had high hopes that she would be his heir, or heir-ess, apparent. So, it came as quite a surprise when, one night in 1968 as the family was sitting down to a supper of homemade chicken pot pie and peach cobbler, Ronnie stated between bites, "I've been accepted to Iowa State—the veterinary college." For a moment, there was total silence. All eyes turned to Vern who was poking at his carrots and peas and turning a deeper shade of red by the minute. Valley, sensing disaster, leapt in.

"We didn't know you'd applied to college, dear," she said, smiling.

"Um," Ronnie replied, looking down, unable to meet the disappointment in her father's eyes. But he wouldn't let her off the hook, which made the younger sisters squirm in their seats and beg to be excused.

"And just how are you going to pay for this college?" he asked, disappointment lacing his words.

"They gave me a full scholarship—tuition, room, board. Everything," Ronnie said proudly.

"Really, darling? That's wonderful!" Valley exclaimed.

Even Vern could not help but be impressed. However, the big elephant in the room—who was going to take over the farm when Vern and Valley were gone—grew larger every minute.

Meanwhile, Vera was silent. She knew something about Ronnie that no one else knew. She had known this about Ronnie for two years, ever since Ronnie birthed Blessing, Sapphire's colt. Vera had watched Ronnie write in her notebook that night, and many nights after, and finally when Ronnie was out on a house call with Vern birthing a set of breech calves, Vera snuck over to Ronnie's bed and pulled out not one, but twenty notebooks full of what Vera assumed was poetry. It had the shape of poetry but it made no sense to her. Vera stuffed the notebooks back where she found them and sat with her back leaning against her sister's bed, pondering. Her sister was a poet, and a pretty good one at that. What should she do? She had kept in touch with the publisher from New York about her own stories. Should she send him some of Veronica's poems and see what he said?

"Why do you need to go off to college anyway?" Vern asked quietly, "Since when isn't the farm enough for you?" What Vern felt, but was unable to express, was his deep sadness that he seemed unable to protect his daughters from the world. He had bought this farm to keep them all safe, but now, one by one, they were peeling off and diving into the chaos that lay beyond. He felt helpless and afraid for his daughters, especially for Ronnie, whom he loved with all his heart.

Ronnie, who had been looking down at her now cold pot pie, brought her gaze directly to her father.

"Times are changing, Vern," she said boldly.

Vern threw his napkin down. "You don't think I know that? You don't think I know? I'm done here," he said and started to leave the room, but Valley stopped him.

"Vern!" she brought him up sharply. "She's young. She has her life ahead of her. What would you have her do?"

"I'd HAVE HER find a nice boy and settle down. But no, they want to run off to college and sleep with black men and smoke pot to fulfill some hideous dream." Then, he looked straight into Ronnie's eyes, his sharp, dark eyes imploring her not to look away. "But by God, I won't watch you follow in your sister's footsteps. You're staying right here where you're safe, where you belong."

Vera watched Ronnie straighten herself against the rungs of her ladder-back chair. Her dark eyes widened and took on a hardness of their own. She looked at her father as he strode out of the room; she didn't say a word. She didn't need to. Vera could hear it loud and clear. Ronnie was gone.

POWER

THE WHOLE COUNTRY SEEMED TO BOIL IN THE LATE 1960S. THE times were turbulent with protests and everyone reaching for power and demanding rights. All the damning rocks of oppression were cast aside as Blacks, gays, lesbians, women, and even children asserted themselves in the face of perceived tyranny. By 1968, when Ronnie was applying to vet school and the younger Books were walking on eggshells around Vern, who seemed to lament every move the girls made, Victoria had dropped out of college and was following Freddie Poole, a member of the Black Panthers, who she had met at a party at college. Freddie seduced her in more ways than one, and before she could even recover from a bad acid trip, she found herself traveling from city to city watching the Civil Rights movement grow. With the assassination of Martin Luther King, Jr. in April of that year, the movement exploded and riots broke out everywhere. Freddie, who saw himself as something of a star in the organization, dragged Victoria down to the headquarters in Baltimore. He stood on an old, wood table, which was anchored in a sea of lime green shag carpeting, fomenting anger, and hatred toward the Oppressors, all of whom were white. Victoria, acutely conscious of the color of her skin, stuck to the corners trying to avoid being noticed. She supported Freddie. She didn't think it was fair, she thought to herself as she looked out through the smoke-filled room and the crowd of animated black faces punching at the air. After all, she supported the cause, but she felt it could never be her cause. As much as she sympathized with the plight of the black people, she was still very white. She could be a feminist, she thought. That was a cause she could hang her hat on. Whatever. She just liked the thrill of being inside that cauldron of seething emotions. She found the anger very much like a drug, and it allowed her to express her own rage and disappointment that she carried inside.

Despite her relating to the movement, she was never really a part of it. Neither the black nor the white women accepted her, and she felt a deadening sense of isolation that she covered up with heavy drinking and drugging until she found out, in June of 1969, as she watched the in-fighting in the Black Panthers movement bring it down, that she was pregnant with Freddie's child.

Much to Victoria's amazement, Freddie was proud, peacock proud, and broadcast the news to anyone who would listen. But Victoria was not so ecstatic. She was ashamed. She didn't want a baby, any baby, when she was so young. Only 20 years old. She thought about getting rid of it, but there were no reasonable options, so she did the only thing she could. Freddie, who seemed more concerned about the mother and child than the mother was, insisted that they marry and then brought Victoria to his mother's home in Benton Harbor, Michigan, where she looked forward to a perfectly awful winter eating ham hocks and learning to crochet. She missed the excitement of being on the road. She missed the riots and the conviction. But Mama Poole, who worked as a domestic for some rich folks in St. Joseph, had a piano in her living room and she encouraged Victoria to play.

Soon she was playing in the local Black church. She played to extravagant hats and vibrant dresses. She played to gleaming white smiles and abundant hugs. She played while her stomach swelled and the baby grew. She came to appreciate the soft, black hands that reached for her stomach to feel the child inside, the dust motes and the doilies. Where before, with the younger Black Panther girls, she had felt ostracized and unwanted, here with Mama Poole and her friends she laughed, listened to Artie Shaw, and lapped up buckets of sweet tea.

In the spring, just before her baby was born, she and Mama Poole took a walk on what was the first spring day of the year. The sun was bright and strong. The smell of rich earth seeped up from the ground, no longer imprisoned by snow. They looked for, and found, purple crocuses and delicate white snowdrops growing near the warm sidewalk. Robins strutted their fat red bellies, and she could relate.

"Are you ready, Sugar? Your life's about to change, forever," Mama Poole said as she held Victoria's hand.

"I'm ready, Mama Poole," she replied. That night she gave birth to a 7lb. 7 oz. baby boy whom she named Artie.

When Freddie came to meet his son the following week, Victoria was gone.

THE GIRL WHO HAD EVERYTHING

IN 1953, THE YEAR THAT THE THIRD BOOK DAUGHTER WAS BORN, Elizabeth Taylor starred in a movie titled *The Girl who had Everything*. The story of a spoiled girl who falls in love and leaves her stable boyfriend for a gangster is not what appealed to Valley and Vern. What caught their attention were the actress's violet eyes; their baby was born with those same eyes. Vern pleaded with Valley to name the child Elizabeth, or even Taylor, to break the chain of "V's" she had begun with the older siblings, a practice too cute for his liking, but Valley insisted that the child be called Violet, or Velvet after Elizabeth Taylor's blockbuster hit *National Velvet*. She tried from the start to ensure that this daughter, so milky in complexion and with those glorious movie-star eyes, would have everything.

Although Valley would never admit it, she did have favorites. Not Victoria, who was haughty and petulant even for a four-year-old, or Veronica who, at two, showed signs of being a tomboy. Violet was the apple of Valley's eye. She was a rare grape, silky and smooth with a pronounced taste. She was an armful of fragrant purple lilacs. She was sweet rose water. Valley couldn't help but adore her.

While Violet was the baby of the family, all coos and cuteness, she thrived on the patting and holding, the loving and adoring. She grew just fat enough to be edible, which is what everyone wanted to do when the beautiful child with the dark, silky hair and violet eyes opened her arms and propelled herself toward them. She was a star. The older children were left in her shadow and Valley made no bones about it. Until one breezy summer afternoon, Vera was born, peaches and cream complexion and brilliant Bachelor's Button blue eyes, white peach fuzz for hair that would later grow into long golden ringlets bouncing against her back. From the minute that Vera entered the scene and stole her mother's affection, Violet began to have health issues. Stomach disorders and fevers accompanied by rashes that came out of nowhere. Her bones seemed to break if someone sneezed. When she was three, she stumbled into the pond and drowned, completely dead, until Vern waded in to the shallow water where she had gulped in death, and resuscitated her. That got Valley's attention. From then on, at least for another year, all eyes were on Violet. Valley made sure that she had everything.

While the two older girls shared a room and Vera was stuffed into what had formerly been used as a linen closet, Violet enjoyed a comfortable space of her own, papered a creamy white studded with tiny violets, luxurious purple drapes that Valley had sewn framing the window that looked out onto the backyard swings and over into the cornfields. Violet was pampered and protected, at great expense; she wandered around the house in dresses with frills and bows like some kind of fancy ghost, always in her mother's shadow while Vera and Veronica, in their hand-me-downs, chased chickens and collected eggs, hunted down tadpoles and earthworms, and hung upside down from the low, and high, branches of trees looking at the world from a different perspective. And still the green grass grew at their heads and the bubbles of clouds sailed lazily by at their feet.

Two more Books were born: Virginia, in 1957, when Violet was four, and Viveca, in 1959, when she was six. By seven years old, Violet had become surly and depressed, which she disguised by being Valley's right-hand helper and friend. She watched the babies so Valley could hang the wash or take a nap, pinching them until they were pocked with white stars. She harvested the vegetables from the garden, spitting on the lettuce and radishes as she prepared salads for her sisters. She purposefully marched her way through each day, determined to make herself indispensable, and then, at night, she would sneak down to the kitchen and eat the leftover chicken thighs or cornbread or, better still, the brownies she had baked and denied herself even one in front of her family, wanting to look the saint, to be the one no one could live without.

The only solace that could soothe Violet's aching heart was the cats. Every farm has cats. Cats that initially start as one or two suddenly multiply. One morning you walk into the barn and there is a congregation of cats—big cats, little cats, gray cats, black cats, mama cats, kittens. Violet loved them all and they loved her in return. When they heard her open the heavy wooden barn door, letting the sun slide in, making shafts of gold, the cats would come running, leaping down from bales of hay where they had hidden happily from other humans and dogs.

KITTENS!

VERA REMEMBERED ONE AFTERNOON WHEN THE KITTENS WERE born. She sauntered over to the barn with nothing to do, thinking that she would maybe help Veronica muck out a stall or lie in the hay bales, arms crossed under her head, and think up a new story. When she got to the barn, the door was closed and it took all her eight-year-old strength to push it wide. As she walked into the barn, sweet with the smell of horses and hay, Ronnie called out to her.

"Close that door!" Vera obeyed as she always obeyed everything Ronnie told her. She ventured into the barn, wiping away sticky cobwebs and looking out for dung.

"Where are you?" she called out.

"Here. Up here," Ronnie answered. Vera looked up and saw her sister, tall at the top of the ladder leading to the hayloft. "Violet has kittens."

Kittens! Vera's heart jumped a beat as she ran toward the ladder and began to scamper up.

"Slow down! You'll scare them," Ronnie barked, which Vera did because she always did everything Ronnie told her. As she reached the top of the ladder, she saw Violet, sitting cross legged in a pretty, blue dress, crowned in a halo of light. She looked like the Virgin

Mary, only in her lap she wasn't holding the Savior of the world but four tiny black kittens, pink eyes bulging, still shut to the world, and a mother cat.

"How does she let you do that?" Vera asked, confused that the mother would share her brood so quickly.

"She trusts me," Violet responded without looking up.

"Can I?" Vera asked, lunging toward Violet's lap.

"She trusts ME," Violet said firmly. "You stay back."

"They aren't just your kittens," Vera stated forcefully.

"They kind of are," Ronnie said, laying her hand on Vera's shoulder. "Let's just look. You can hold them another time."

The three sisters sat and watched the sleeping black kittens that looked like baby moles or rats. *When you're that small*, Vera thought, *no one can tell you apart from, say, a walnut.* But it was peaceful in the barn with the silence and the dust motes showering down in the light.

"What are you going to name them?" Vera asked, breaking into the quiet.

"John, Paul, George, and Ringo," Violet replied quickly.

"Cool," Vera grinned. "But what if they're girls?"

"We'll call them John, Paul, George, and Ringo. What's wrong with that?" Ronnie asked.

"We will not!" Violet cried. "We'll call them Joan, Paulette, Georgina, and Ringo-beth." Ronnie rolled her eyes. They were quiet again for a while; then, once again, Vera broke the ice.

"How will you tell them apart?" she asked.

"I'll know," Violet replied. "A mother knows."

"But you're not …" Vera began, but she stopped as Ronnie pinched her younger sister's elbow.

"She kind of is," Ronnie said quietly.

Vera stood rigidly for several minutes brooding on this situation. Here was Violet, yet again, hogging a moment, taking a good thing, and claiming it was all her own. She did it with Valley. She did it with space. She did it with time. Now she was doing it with the kittens. Vera, who was tired of being denied and shoved into a little box, could no longer take the frustration. She lunged at the kittens and pulled one out of Violet's lap.

"You're not! You're not their mother and this is as much mine as it is yours!" she cried, holding the kitten firmly under her chin.

Violet said nothing. She stared at Vera, breathing loudly and more loudly, as if bellowing fire to come out of her mouth. When she finally did speak, it was with a venom and fierceness unbecoming a child, especially one in a blue dress with a halo of light circling her head.

"I hate you," she said quietly. "I hate you. HATE you. HATE YOU!" she said louder and louder.

Vera felt a lump swell up in her chest. She had always known that Violet didn't like her, but never had she felt that truth with such a certainty as now. Before the tears could start pouring out and she would begin heaving with loneliness and despair, she put the kitten gently in Violet's lap, turned and descended the ladder, walked out of the barn, and then ran like hell to her very small room where she cried and cried, messy, snotty, tears that burned and scarred. *She hates me. They hate me. She hates me.*

She would feel it, many years later, long after they had made peace with each other, as if Violet had taken a fiery hot branding iron and pressed it into her soul. *She hates me*, whispered the small voice that came from a lonely girl sitting on a giant rock in a swirling stream. *She hates me.* It would never go away.

CAMOUFLAGE

THE FIFTH LITTLE CHAPTER IN THE BOOK FAMILY, AS VALLEY HAD lately taken to saying when referring to her offspring, was Virginia. She was named Virginia because of the perfectly triangular birthmark, the shape of the state by the same name, Valley's home state, which decorated a positively adorable little hip. Vera always thought that Virginia was the most beautiful of the sisters, not because she was the thinnest or was the most classic looking or had a sensational head of hair. She didn't. She was rather ordinary looking with her wavy brown hair, which she would later call mousey and dye, and her plain brown eyes, neither chocolate nor amber, nothing sensational like Violet's or Vera's own, which she would later disguise under colored contact lenses.

But Virginia had something, spirit, spunk if you will. She enjoyed who she was and she enjoyed every second of life. Maybe because by the time she was born, Valley had given up on expectations and hopes. She just let Virginia be who she was: a goofy little girl who loved to dance and twirl and sing popular songs at the top of her lungs.

When she was two, she took Valley's hand and led her outside to see the "Glowies." Valley had no idea what the "Glowies" were, but she let the child lead her down the porch steps and across the dew-covered lawn to the lattice arch that stood at the entrance of the vegetable garden. Climbing up the latticework were slender green vines decorated with the bright blue bells of morning glories. Virginia let go of Valley's hand and toddled as fast as she could to the flowers. "Glowies!" she cried. And then she kissed the ones that she could reach, standing tippy toes on her sturdy legs, wishing each "Morning!" Valley's heart ached as it did so often with Virginia.

At ten years old, Virginia returned on a train from Boston where she had spent time with her Uncle Mike and Aunt Arlene and the cousins who had visited the year before and had fallen in love with the precocious child. She was wearing a black and white op-art plastic dress that her aunt had bought for her, and green vinyl go-go boots. Across her shoulder was slung a green vinyl pocketbook suspended on a gold loop chain, a pocketbook that held a small plastic comb, a miniature bottle of Chantilly perfume, a packet of Juicy Fruit gum, a zippo lighter, and a pack of Parliaments, which she had stolen from her generous aunt's purse. Two weeks with her wealthy relatives had made Virginia a changed girl. No one knew, except Vera, that, in Massachusetts, egged on by her older cousins, Virginia had taken up the bad habit that her mother indulged in. Careful to erase the smell with mouthwash, gum, and perfume, she tolerated Vern calling her Pepe le Pew as long as the scents camouflaged her secret.

The only reason Vera knew was that one night, when she was sitting in the loft thinking up a new story, she smelled something burning and thought the barn might be on fire. She got up to look around and discovered Virginia, crouched down by a pile of manure, puffing away.

"What are you doing?" Vera asked brusquely.

"What does it look like I'm doing?" Virginia quipped back.

"You know you could burn the barn down," Vera warned.

"I'm being careful," Virginia stated, emphasizing her point by flicking ashes into a bucket of water.

"What if Vern finds out?"

"He won't, if you don't tell him," Virginia said, taking a deep drag on her cigarette and then exhaling a slow, steady plume of smoke. "Want a drag?" she asked, offering Vera the cigarette.

"Yuk." Vera scrunched her nose. "C'mon. Let's get out of here."

"Alright." Virginia took one more drag, and then extinguished the stub with a hiss. She put the soggy butt in her pocket and the two left the barn and walked out into the sunlight.

"Wait a minute," the younger sister exclaimed as she dug a hole and planted the butt, covering it up carefully to avoid drawing attention to it.

As the sisters walked toward the house, they were both very quiet, each heavy with questions to ask the other. "How long?" Vera blurted out while Virginia chimed in "You won't" simultaneously.

"I won't tell Vern, but you have to promise me you won't smoke in the barn."

"I promise," Virginia said though she knew she probably would.

"And I won't tell Vern. Promise," Vera agreed, and she knew that she wouldn't break that promise, not out of loyalty or dedication to her sister but rather because the writer in her wanted to see how all of this would play out.

AWAY IN A MANGER

CHRISTMAS EVE, AND THE BOOKS ARE BUSY PREPARING FOR Christmas. Vern and Ronnie lug in the tree, a fat, fragrant spruce that set Vern back more than he would have liked. But Valley had insisted on the extravagance, stating that Christmas only comes once a year and it was important to make memories that the girls could hold on to all their lives. While Vern and Ronnie were gone, Valley had assembled the remaining four—Victoria was at church practicing for the evening service—in a line from the attic steps to the corner of the living room where the tree would stand, fully decorated, for the world to see. Not that anyone ever came by, but in case they did, and so that, Virginia reminded them all, Santa could see that their house was ready for him to drop a sleigh load of presents under the tree. Vera, who had now caught on to the fact that there really was no Santa Claus, that Valley and Vern were the elves who bought and hid throughout the Christmas season, smiled knowingly at Valley, who put her finger to her lips.

So, there they were, lined up like a fire brigade, passing boxes of fragile ornaments from one small child to the next. When Viveca, only three at the time, tripped and would have fallen while holding a box of straw ornaments, Valley saw the error of her plan. She sat Viveca down with some coloring books and crayons to occupy her until later in the festivities. And how many festivities there were! There was the tree decorating, hanging the balls carefully on the boughs after Vern had strung the fat, colored bulbs that shone loud and bright over the tree. Once the wooden nutcrackers were on, and the plastic Snoopy ornaments and candy canes, the girls sprinkled silver tinsel that fell like icicles, catching the blue, green, yellow, and red lights on their surfaces and shimmering like fire. Viveca, who simply grabbed handfuls of the silver stuff and threw it at the tree where it rested, clumped in a ball, knotted and thick, was escorted back to the crayon table where she marked every page with a golden X, pouting just a little.

As the children decorated the tree, Valley baked cookies, hundreds of cookies—Snicker doodles and Lace cookies, peanut butter drops with Hershey's Kisses in the center and sugar cookies cut out in all shapes and sizes for the girls to decorate. The house smelled like sugar, warm and sweet, as the girls ran to the kitchen table to create masterpieces of red and green icing with silver balls and rainbow sprinkles that ran off their plates like mercury and fell to the kitchen floor. Viveca got down on all fours and pressed her tongue to the floor, licking up sprinkles like a dog. Valley scooped her up and sat her in a chair at the table with the big girls, placing a giant cookie shaped like a bell in front of her with some frosting and a plastic knife, stating "Decorate!" But Viveca just slipped out of her seat, ran to the coloring table, and began to scribble in a purple donkey standing at Jesus's birth.

Hours later, after the cookies were all finished and heaped on plates or tied to the tree, after the kitchen was cleaned and the ruckus of Christmas carols on the radio and children squeaking and squealing and fighting over who thought to decorate that way first, after Vern had made a fire in the fireplace and settled in front of it with a bottle and a drink, and Valley had set the table for a delicious meal of homemade macaroni and cheese, ham, green bean casserole, and biscuits, did anyone notice that Viveca was gone.

"When did you last see her?" Valley asked the girls as she raced, scattered, around the kitchen and living room, opening cupboards and closets, hoping that Viveca was hiding somewhere there.

"She probably took herself upstairs for a nap," Vern yelled from his chair in front of the fire, remaining infuriatingly calm, in Valley's estimation.

Violet ran up to the girl's bedroom to look. "She's not here!" she yelled as she came dashing back.

"Oh, my God, the pond!" Valley cried as she swept toward the front door, pulling out a flashlight and grabbing a sweater as she went. This couldn't be happening again, she thought. Another child near death or dead in this puddle of water that Vern insisted on keeping. She ran toward the water calling, "Viveca! Viveca! Where are you?" Vern, who had gotten up from his chair and grabbed a flashlight of his own, joined her. Together they swept their lights over the dark water, but they saw nothing.

"She's not in there any way," Vern said stoically.

"How do you know? She could have sunk," Valley lamented.

"If she drowned, she'd be floating on the top," Vern stated, which, oddly enough, gave Valley a little comfort.

As they walked slowly back from the pond, Valley saw the door to the barn was open and a light was shining through.

"Of course! The barn!" she cried, letting go of Vern's hand and running toward the open door. Sure enough, inside she found Ronnie with her baby sister, who was lying in a trough filled with straw, sound asleep. She looked so peaceful there, a secret smile on her lips, her little hands balled tight under her chin. Almost as if on cue, she opened her eyes and looked up at her parents and sister standing above her. "Is he here yet?" she asked.

"No," Valley smiled, "Santa's not here yet."

"Not him," Viveca said petulantly. "Baby Jesus. Is Baby Jesus here yet?"

Valley never forgot that story about Viveca, not for one minute, not one detail. Swept away as she was, the other girls were, in the jolly holiday aspect of Christmas, caught up in the distractions of the lights, camera, action of the merry and bright, she had somewhere put the Jesus thing on the back burner. In a way, she felt humbled by her three-year-old child who grew, through life, to be a girl of quiet faith. Valley didn't really know where it came from. Neither she nor Vern were really church goers. They tended to believe more in a Universal Power than Jesus Himself, but not so for Viveca. She had a special connection, a personal relationship with Jesus that sustained her throughout her life. She had been touched by Grace, and that was all there was to it.

THE GIRL IN THE MIRROR

THE FOURTH SISTER, VERA BOOK, HAD HER NOSE IN EVERYONE'S business, and for that reason she was the least popular of all the Book girls, at least among her sisters. They would find her spying on them when they were making out with their boyfriends or stealing a cigarette in the barn. Once, Violet caught Vera standing in her closet, peering out, as she tried to squeeze herself into a sun dress that fit her several dozen donuts ago but now made the fat on her back lump together when she tried to do up the zipper. Vera always seemed to come upon her sisters at their worst moments, picking their noses or eating their toenails, and then, to their dismay, she would take out her notebook and pen and start writing.

What she wrote, they could only imagine, for no one had ever managed or dared to read the secrets she kept. They all assumed she had written the worst, because they believed that she was just that. The worst. Malicious. Vindictive. Mean.

No one else saw Vera that way. To them she was an angel with blonde curls and dancing blue eyes and a serious smile that added to her charm. As a little girl, she sat in her father's lap and batted her dark eyelashes and won him over. The men at church couldn't get enough of this cupcake of a child, and she learned very early how to manipulate a crowd, standing on the shoes of older men as they waltzed her around the room, allowed to stay up later than the other girls.

But all that special treatment left her with nothing but a hole in her heart. She knew that she could persuade her parents and their friends of anything. What Vera did not know was that she had no control over her life, and soon the hollow ache inside her would take over and she would try to fill it at first by looking, then by stealing, then by drinking.

Vera looked everywhere for things that might fill her—Nature, books, writing, everywhere, anywhere, anything to make her feel if not loved then whole. Looking brought nothing and shimmied into stealing. She stole Violet's cherry-print underpants. She stole Victoria's green felt cloche. She stole Veronica's Tennessee walker horse model. She scaled a dresser and a chair to get to the top of Valley's closet where she found a beige rubber diaphragm that repulsed her so she got down and filched a pair of earrings from her mother's jewelry box instead. And then, Vera buried them all in a shoe box in the barn, like a serial killer, so she could take them out and be with them. Only the hole in her soul did not go away.

When she was 12, she began stealing Vern's liquor. The bitter tasting gin which she had assumed would taste like water but which made her gag the first time she swallowed it. The sweet sherry that tickled her nose. The bourbon that went down like fire. All of it, enough of it, took away the edge of anxiety and loneliness she lived in every day. She'd invite Peaches Rickey, her best friend, over to the farm where they would alternate swigs from the bottle of bourbon that she filched from her parents' cabinets. Or Peaches would come over with some Boone's Farm, easier to take though sickly. They'd laugh and talk and for a moment, Vera felt connected. The empty hole would vanish. But as soon as the buzz wore off and Peaches had disappeared down the road on her bike, the hole was back. And so, Vera stole regularly, careful to replenish with water, until by the time she was 14 and her parents felt that she was old enough to have a glass of wine with dinner, Vera was already drinking daily and a lot.

LOSING CAMELOT

For most people, November 22, 1963, began as just another day. For the Book sisters, it meant jostling for space at the bathroom sink to get faces washed and teeth brushed while the sky was still dark and they made their preparations for school. The colder weather called for bulkier outfits, flannel-lined jeans, turtlenecks, and sweaters. They wore knee-high socks and jackets and even gloves for the mile-long walk to the bus stop under the starry sky, a walk generally punctuated by bickering between Vera and Violet, refereed by Veronica, and slammed to a stop by Victoria, who wasn't about to be embarrassed in front of her high-school friends by her little sisters arguing over who stole whose underpants or some similar topic. This morning, though, the girls were quiet. Vera was concentrating on the clouds her breath made when she exhaled and looking up into the vast morning sky, wondering where infinity stopped if it stopped at all. Violet had snuck a kitten into her coat pocket and was coaxing it to sleep by tickling it under the chin. Veronica was just quiet, in the moment, while Victoria's mind forged ahead, wondering when she could escape this prison that was her life and hoping that Sheila, her new best friend, had snuck some gin in her thermos so at least there was lunchtime to look forward to.

Earlier, while Vern fed the horses, chickens, cats and cow in the barn, Vera ate a bowl of Lucky Charms, carefully extracting the marshmallows and saving them up for last while Valley pulled at her tangled hair until she could make a braid that hung like a fat rope against Vera's back. Lunches were lined up neatly in a row, all the same: peanut butter-and-jelly sandwiches, an apple, and a sack of carrot sticks. Milk they would buy in the cafeteria with the nickel Valley gave each of them as they marched out the door. Little did Valley know that the only one who ate anything was Violet. The rest tossed their lunches in the trash, going without, or traded, as Vera did, for a quarter to buy an ice-cream sandwich from the tall vending machines in the cafeteria.

The day for Vera was mundane. Hours spent practicing penmanship in workbooks with dotted lines and no pictures. Time devoted to reading about the adventures of Dick and Jane, which were not really adventures at all but monosyllabic fabrications of the Life of an American Boy and Girl and their Dog, Spot. Vera used the time to daydream. What if she did have a dog? She would like a big dog, like the dog on "Top Hat," a dog that you could really lose yourself in and play around with. A dog that she would name Hero. Her Hero. But they couldn't have a dog because Virginia was allergic to their dander. None of it was fair, she thought as she drew a moustache on Jane with her pencil and then quickly erased it as Miss Bloom came by. Math was next, with its colored abacuses which were supposed to help her with her problems but which only confused her more. Still, she liked playing with the colored beads and the painted fraction blocks because they were pretty, like rainbows, so she didn't mind.

At recess, she was the one to take the new erasers to the monster machine that sucked all the chalk out of them, making them ready for a few more hours of work. Only this day, November 22, 1963, there would not be another few hours of work. This day the principal came to the classroom door and had a brief, hushed conversation with Miss Bloom, who turned back to the class ashen-faced and told them all to clean up their desks and pack their things, they were going home early. As the voice that came over the loudspeaker explained, "The president has been shot. President Kennedy is dead."

Even in her eight-year-old mind, Vera knew that this was obviously a catastrophic event. She had listened to Valley and Vern, mostly Valley, rave about the handsome, young, Catholic president who was doing such good things for the country. She had applauded his decision to run for a second term. Valley's dream was to take all her girls to the White House to meet the beautiful Jacqueline Kennedy and see how she had so wonderfully decorated the mansion with fabrics, furniture, and fine art from all over the world. Valley's hope was that her children would grow up to play with John, Jr. and Caroline, and that some of the Kennedy poise and flair would rub off on her daughters, who had lived all their lives on a farm. These were the ideas Valley shared with the young Book girls as she tucked them into bed at night, hoping to fill their heads with happy dreams.

But now, President Kennedy was dead and Jackie was a widow and John and Caroline would grow up without a father. All because of someone's hate. And that made Vera cry. She cried at her desk with her head in her arms until her best friend, Peaches Rickey, came over and put her arms around Vera and cried too. The little girls cried all the way to Peaches' house where they sat in front of the TV watching and re-watching the enactment of the day's events, all the while dipping chocolate chip cookies into cold milk and stuffing their sorrow and their fear.

For the kids, it was an almost abstract occurrence, something they knew was serious enough to shut down school for a day and set all the flags at half-mast. For Valley, it was as if Lee Harvey Oswald had taken his gun and pointed it directly at her. With Kennedy's death, a big part of Valley died too. Her optimism, her hope, her willingness to believe that the world could be a good place, all left her. Lethargy seeped in and she began to smoke heavily and drink, and contemplate what it would be like to be with another man.

Losing her dream of "Camelot" had left Valley with no dream at all. She suddenly felt hopelessly trapped in her limited existence, made smaller by lack of funds to do anything about it. Yet she was too depressed to work. The little bit of money that she had been making as a freelance journalist dribbled away. She felt bullied by circumstances, as if she had been the one who was left a widow, and in a way, she had been. Vern was taking the assassination almost as hard as she. The event brought back fears that he had been trying to escape since the war. These fears led him to project the future and forecast disaster, so he drank. He drank to turn off both the memories and the nightmares. He drank regularly until, gradually, he drank not to escape the monsters of the past and future but simply out of habit.

Valley would have liked to have written a letter to someone, anyone, God especially, expressing how she felt, but she wasn't sure where to send it. Still, she wrote anyway, a short, heartfelt letter to Jackie Kennedy. And then notes to the children, separately. Then, she wrote to the governor of Texas and to the head of the Secret Service. She stayed up late at night, a cigarette in the ashtray sending smoke into the still air, a glass of whiskey next to her, ice cubes melting, chinking, and she wrote. She continued to write for years to come, protesting the many injustices she witnessed, applauding the actions and courage of some. The letters were her circular buoys, the lifelines that kept her from drowning as she watched the world unravel around her while she, powerless to the onslaught of Time, fell deeper and deeper into the whirlpool. Vera watched her from the shadows, peering around the open door, heavy with sadness as she watched her mother slip away.

DOWN IN THE VALLEY

VALLEY WAS SLUMPED DOWN IN THE MUSTARD-COLORED NAUGAHYDE recliner drinking Scotch and smoking cigarettes as she watched the news on the black-and-white television. Children no older than her own chanted "Peace" while impersonal police officers wearing helmets with visors so dark you could not see their eyes and wielding shields and batons like gladiators met and struggled and fought. It seemed the war in Vietnam would never end, though rumor had it troops would be withdrawn soon.

She was glad that she had only borne girls. They had been spared the agony of the lottery and deployment and return of sons, maimed physically and mentally, or dead in a wooden box. The Shepherd's son Alex had met such a fate. And Julie Shepherd, Valley's friend from the flower guild at church, had taken it hard. She blamed her husband, Nolan, for not letting the boy run away to Canada, for insisting that "no Shepherd has ever been a coward," and rubbing that message into his young son's face until the boy couldn't say no. He signed up, and left, and within a week was gone.

A week after his burial in the town cemetery where too many flags waved over fresh graves, Julie drove off to California with some Flower Children who had somehow mistakenly ended up at the church. She had no other children and only bitterness in her heart for Nolan who never shed a tear until one afternoon when he was drinking Scotch with Valley and it all began.

Valley never meant to fall into an affair with Nolan. She loved Vern. She loved her life on the farm. But these were confusing times, times of great achievement and promise—men stepping out onto the Moon—half a million, young people congregating at the Woodstock festival. But they were also hard times for Valley and Vern.

Victoria, who had gone off to Oberlin on a music scholarship in 1967, got pregnant not by Barton Barkley, the pianist she had been seeing clandestinely, but by another black man who called himself a Brother and claimed that Victoria was a witch who had cast a spell over him. Boldly, he led rallies, inciting anger and violence in his Black Brothers and Sisters. How Victoria fit into all of this, Valley could not understand. How had her Victoria, the musical prodigy, ended up dropping out of music school and traipsing around with a radical Black man? When Victoria called Valley in 1969 with the news that she was pregnant, Valley couldn't even pretend to be glad. She saw her oldest daughter's life taking a terrible turn, a forever turn. But Victoria swelled with her first born, trapped by circumstance, until finally she gave birth in 1970 to a mulatto boy.

"The gingerbread child," Vern called him, shaking his head. "Who'd have thought I'd have a black grandson," he commented as he popped the tab on his Schlitz, his beer of choice, the seventh that afternoon. "The times sure are a changing."

It was in 1969 that Ronnie left veterinary school after only one year of study. She had decided that she would make a go of it in Greenwich Village. At least, that's what she told Valley and Vern. The truth was, she had become addicted to cocaine at vet school and was joining a group that abstained from drugs altogether. This was a secret she would carry to her grave, she believed, until she spilled the beans when Vera was concerned about Vern's drinking.

In 1970, Valley watched the family fall apart: Victoria with her pregnancy and no hope of an abortion; Ronnie with her "group of poets" which turned out to be just a cluster of sober friends; Vern drinking more and more over the state of the world, the state of the farm, the state of his daughters, and most of all the state of his marriage. Valley knew that even though he didn't know about the affair, he suspected something but had to tell himself it wasn't true.

Meanwhile, Valley convinced herself that she was doing a good thing, bringing comfort to a man who had lost his son and his wife in one week. She let herself deliberately believe that this was the truth because if she didn't, if she saw herself for what she really was, she would have to acknowledge that, loose times or not, she was an adulteress and no one wants to hear that about herself.

While Valley philandered and Vern declined, drinking beer and the watered-down liquor that Vera stole, Violet cooked and cleaned and ate until she blew up like an exercise ball, coy and giggling as she licked off the eggbeaters covered in brownie mix or sucked out the insides of Oreos, drowning her denial in gallons of milk that she claimed were good for her teeth and bones. Virginia, who was up to a pack of cigarettes a week now, and hiding it, and Viveca, who seemed to be the only sane one in the family, whispered behind her back that Violet no longer had bones. She was just a giant jellyfish made of jelly donuts and crème horns.

There was so much denial in the Book household in 1969 that everyone was fine. There was nothing wrong. It was the times, they were a changing. And so were the Books, changing, until they could barely recognize themselves. And when they did, what they saw they didn't like at all.

WHERE THERE IS SMOKE

OF ALL THE EVENTS THAT TOOK PLACE IN THE EARLY 1970S—THE Kent State shootings, Watergate, the escalation of the Vietnam War—Valley Book was most concerned about the ban on cigarette advertisements on TV. Suddenly, the severity of Valley's "bad habit" was brought to her family's attention. While before it had been a nuisance, waved away by disapproving hands and countered by open windows and fans, now her smoking was being referred to as an addiction, one that could result in cancer, or even death.

Valley didn't want to give up smoking. Some of the happiest moments for her were after she and Nolan had sex and they passed a cigarette back and forth between them, sensually inhaling and exhaling the calming drug. She imagined herself to be a seductive movie star like Marlene Dietrich or Lauren Bacall, glancing up at her lover through half-veiled eyes, looking at him through a dull haze.

When Valley cut down on the smoking, she cut down on Nolan too. None of it was working anyway, not the sex, not the smoking, not the drinking. She was wrapped in depression like a piece of leftover meat in plastic wrap or a prisoner of war with a black hood awaiting execution. Life was too difficult, too damned difficult, and none of her drugs worked.

Vern, meanwhile, was tortured by what he saw in his fields. Ear rot on the corn, sprung up overnight, had rotted the husks from the inside out. When he touched the blighted ears, they fell to pieces, showering like chalk dust to the too moist ground. Vern's was not the only crop hit. Farms all around were suffering the same damage from what the press was now calling Southern Corn Leaf Blight. Mercifully, the past three years had been lucrative and solvent, so Vern was in no danger of losing his farm this year, despite heavy losses. But if the blight persisted, if it did not disappear, who knew? His farm, his livelihood, his whole way of life could vanish. Then what would he do? Projecting into the amber bubbles in his bottle of beer, he found the solution. Send the women away for a spell so he could think, and drink, in peace. He needed space from Valley anyway. Though he knew the affair with Nolan had run its course and was now done, he needed time to think, and drink, in peace. He told himself this as he rocked in the old wooden chair on the porch. Think, drink, peace.

So, Valley took the four younger Book sisters to Woolsama, Minnesota, to spend a month at Peace Lake. The older girls would be there for the entire summer, working as chambermaids at the resort, while the younger two, spoiled as they were, would drink Shirley Temples by the water, canoe, play horseshoes, swim, and generally have fun. That was all right with Vera. She and Violet were assigned a small lakeside cabin where they could cook, and eat, and entertain however their hearts desired. Vera wasn't entirely convinced that living with Violet was going to be a good thing, but she was willing to give it a try. Anything was better than being at home with Vern drinking his sorrows away and taking it out on them, or Valley sneaking around trying to hide the fact that she was still smoking like a chimney, just not inside. Anything would be better than the thick film of denial they put up to avoid talking about Victoria, who was divorced and trolling for a man to marry. Or Veronica, who had taken a lover, the leader of the poets' cluster, a woman with long red curls and flashing green eyes who called herself Wren.

Vern denounced both daughters in a drunken stupor one night, disowned them and threatened to shoot them if they ever walked through the kitchen door. Then, wielding a butcher knife, he threatened the four younger Books, warning them that if he ever caught one of them stepping out of line, he'd take this knife, he said, gesturing with it wildly, and cut them to pieces like cheese for fondue and feed them to Miss Maybelline, an image which sent Viveca and Virginia running into the folds of Valley's apron, bawling. Violet, meanwhile, was fighting back tears and gulping, trapped in her own fantasy, while Vera stood tall with her arms crossed, daring her father to take a step. Daring him to give her a reason to leave and never come back.

A week later, the Book women formed a little caravan driving to Minnesota. Valley took the big tan station wagon with the seats pulled down in the "way back" so the twins could enjoy a comfortable ride. Violet and Vera followed in a bright orange Ford Pinto, a gift from Vern who felt remorse and shame over too many things to enumerate, but one of them was being a bad father. The girls accepted the car without comment, packed what they could in the small vehicle because Violet had taken up half the back seat with a cat crate for Glorioso, her huge, fluffy, gray monstrosity who she insisted would languish without her for three months. The rest of their stuff went on Valley's roof.

"We can do this," Vera said to Violet, who looked skeptical about driving on unfamiliar roads all the way to Minnesota with someone who had only had her license for about a day. "We can do this," Vera repeated. "It'll be great," though secretly she wondered if traveling 680 miles with a carsick cat and an anxious, claustrophobic, overweight girl was really such a good idea. Not to mention, she had only just passed her driving test.

The trip was mostly made without conversation. Vera had set the dial to a radio station that played almost non-stop music, and the girls chugged along the highway singing along with the lyrics of the day—Deep Purple's "Smoke on the Water," Rod Stewart's "You Wear It Well," Elton John's "Rocket Man," Alice Cooper's "School's Out," and Neil Young's "Heart of Gold" were played over and over again.

"I love Neil Young," said Violet, who had been silent for the longest time, except for singing. She had a lovely voice, crystal clear, high and delicate, but she didn't sing often because she didn't like to bring attention to herself, a fat girl with a small voice. Vera thought Jim Nabors, goofy as he was, had an amazing voice. For a moment, she felt compassion for her sister, a nightingale trapped inside a big body, and then Violet continued, "His voice is so plaintive. It makes me sad and depressed. It's comforting."

Oddly enough, Vera knew just what Violet was talking about. There was a way that a sad song could make you feel ok about yourself because it affirmed who you were.

"That's how I feel about Joni Mitchell's entire *Blue* album," Vera confessed. "I wish I could just float away on a river."

"We're kind of floating away now, sort of," Violet giggled.

Vera smiled. She felt a small chink open in her heart to Violet, though she knew she needed to be careful in case Violet slammed it shut again.

"How did we end up hating each other anyway?" Violet asked innocently.

Vera's head swarmed with answers. Because you were a little Bitch Queen who wanted all the attention and I was forced to sleep in a tiny closet. Because you made all the rules about how we were to act around Valley, the kittens, the kitchen, and, God forbid what would happen if we did not obey you? Because you swelled up like a puffer fish and took all of Valley's worry while I am here slowly drinking myself to death and playing with razors and knives. Vera felt her hands gripping the steering wheel tightly. Her heart was racing in her chest.

"We don't hate each other. I don't hate you anyway. We've grown. We've matured. Let's not dwell on the past." And she turned up the radio to blare out the awkward silence, to erase the bad feelings like a smudge stick so they could move on.

A simple melody, clear as a mountain brook, flowed off the radio, and with the light keys ascending the scale showered down lyrics that pierced both girls' hearts. "*What a friend you are/if I had a golden star/ I'd pin it on you/for seeing it through/with me.*" Violet reached over and pressed her hand around Vera's as it gripped the steering wheel. Vera glanced over at Violet and saw that she was crying. "*What a special friend/just the kind who'll never bend/ or break away ....*"

By now, both girls were crying, but for very different reasons. Violet was crying because she felt she had a friend in her sister, someone who loved her for who she was, despite the past, despite the present, Violet took Vera's tears to mean that she cared. But Vera cried not because she cared, but because she couldn't care. She couldn't get over the hurdles of past hurts. She wasn't as simple as Violet, for whom a song could cure everything. She didn't know what it would take to fill the hole in her heart, if anything ever could, so she cried and let her sister believe that it was all alright.

When the song was done, Violet turned off the radio. "Vera," she began, "I'm sorry for the way I was ...."

"It's OK. It's been hard for all of us," Vera replied quickly.

"You are special to me," Violet went on.

"Stop! Just stop. I can't get into all this family stuff now. I need to concentrate on the road."

The road, in fact, had become more demanding now that they were off the straight, flat highway. Plus, they had been driving for almost ten hours and Vera was starting to feel the exhaustion set in. She rolled down the window to let the cool air refresh her. Only then did she really look around to notice the landscape that surrounded them. Trees cradled each side of the road, tall, old trees with magnificent lacey green foliage that fanned the air in the breeze. To the side of the road was a bank that led down to a stream which ran like ribbon candy through the woods. It was a magical forest full of dark green pines and sprawling ferns and dotted with clusters of white daisies. Vera could hear birds over the loud chugging of the car. Along the road ahead was a guardrail to keep enchanted travelers from going over the edge into the ravine below.

As Vera looked at the road ahead, particularly at her mother maneuvering the large station wagon over the curvy road, she sensed that something was wrong. Valley was not slowing down as she came to the turn; if anything, she was accelerating.

"What's she doing?" Vera said aloud.

"Who?" Violet asked.

"Valley. She's not slowing down," Vera stated, alarm in her voice.

"What?" Violet screamed. "Oh, my God!" she shrieked as Valley drove straight into the guardrail on the curve. All the suitcases went flying off the top of the car like a flock of cranes as the station wagon teetered precariously over the edge of the road, tethered only by the thick steel band.

Luckily, no one was hurt. When the police officer who arrived on the scene asked Valley to tell him what had happened, she smiled regretfully and admitted that she was trying to light a smoke, that she had just looked away for a minute. The officer was not taken in by Valley's charm. He looked at her seriously, wrote out a hefty ticket, and as he handed it to her said, "Those things will kill you."

Violet stood with her arm around her sisters, sobbing, while the younger sisters held each other, weeping and repeating, "We could have been killed." Vera retrieved the suitcases, shoving clothes back into the broken bags. With nettles stinging her bare legs and rocks piercing through her thin sandals, she told herself that she would leave this circus quickly, this circus where people seemed so intent on killing themselves, and others.

PEACE

LAKE PEACE ITSELF WAS HEAVEN—SMALL, COMFORTABLE IN SIZE,
bordered by trees all around except where the smooth, green lawns
stretched up to the main resort, a big, wood structure with a vast
wrap-around porch dotted with bright, white rocking chairs. Guests
sat in gaily colored Adirondack chairs on the lawns, sipping drinks
or just resting their heads back, soaking up the sun. Shiny green
canoes cut through the placid water and small children wearing
puffy orange life preservers shaped like horseshoes leaned out of
boats, letting the Jello-smooth water skim beneath their hands.

Amazingly enough, the place was very quiet. The shrieks of
guests entering the icy water for the first time, the whoops of victory
at the horseshoe pit, the cry of a mother looking for a lost child, all
seemed to dissolve into the abundant blue sky and the dense trees.
All Vera could hear were crickets and birds. And in the evening, fat
bellied frogs that croaked in the darkness.

Vera loved the mornings before they went to work. She and
Violet had made a pact that she, Vera, would not drink alcohol for
the three months they were at the lake and that Violet would eat
only vegetables and fruit with a little meat. Her goal was to lose 40
pounds. Every day they walked down to the small dock that jutted

out from the lawn in front of their cabin, with Glorioso following behind them, tiptoeing across the dew and finally settling at the end of the dock like a gray statue as he watched the girls swim a half mile out and a half mile back in the icy water. At first it was gruesome, the water was so cold that it pinched, but gradually the sisters grew to love their morning ritual. Vera loved the clarity with which she began her day. She had even picked up her writing again and was certain that a story would come soon. Violet loved the way that her clothes were starting to get loose, falling off her even, and how her face began to have shadows in the hollows beneath her cheek bones.

Though the hours and the work were grueling—there were only a handful of chambermaids for the entire resort—the girls did manage to have fun, especially once Valley and the twins returned home, though their presence at Lake Peace was hardly noticed. In the month they were there, Vera only ran into her little sisters a few times, and that was always at the soft serve ice cream stand across the street from the resort.

"What are you doing here?" Vera asked Virginia and Viveca when she first saw them standing in line for cones.

"What does it look like?" Virginia responded, typically.

"Valley gave us money for cones. It's ok. We'll be safe," Viveca piped up. "I'm 13 and she's 15. We are old enough to get ice cream on our own."

Vera thought for a moment. She hadn't ever considered how old her sisters were, they were just younger, and indulged, and as Cat Stevens said, "It's a bad world," so she wanted them to be safe. But hey, she told herself, if they want to go off on their own, so be it. It was, after all, only ice cream.

"Are you having a good time here?" Vera asked, changing the subject.

"It's boring. There's nothing to do. It's all old people and little kids," Virginia whined.

"I like it. It's nice. Peaceful," Viveca added.

"Yeah, well just be glad you're not making beds and cleaning toilets all day," Vera laughed, though she knew that was not the extent of their "vacation." There were days off. And there were boys.

Busboys. Grounds keepers. Lifeguards. Waiters. Not all of them were good looking, but each one surpassed Vera's expectations in some way, except for one. He was a tall, lean, tan boy with exceptionally white teeth and a mane of thick, black hair. He was the Chief Lifeguard and he strutted around clad only in his red trunks, his flip flops, and his whistle, flirting with all the girls and saving lives.

The first day that she and Violet arrived, they swam and dried off, put their long hair up in buns, and donned their hideous peach-colored uniforms with the white Peter Pan collars and their white shoes. Old lady shoes, Violet called them. As they walked over to the main resort to get their assignments, the lean boy in the red shorts trotted up beside them. Though it was only eight in the morning and the air was still chilled, he was bare-chested with the whistle hanging like a medal around his neck.

"You girls new?" he asked congenially.

Vera and Violet smiled shyly. How not to be silenced by such a glorious specimen who smelled of Coppertone and radiated the sun? Then, he opened his mouth again.

"I'm Brad," he said holding out his hand. "Chief Lifeguard. And you must be Beauty," he said looking at Vera, "and the Beast," he motioned to Violet.

Both girls were struck dumb by his remark. Vera, who usually had something pithy to say, could think of no retort except to mutter under her breath, "Asshole," as she grabbed Violet by the arm and led her away. Violet burst into tears which had to come to a stop, Vera told her, because how would it look on their first day?

Not all the boys were such assholes. In fact, one of them took up a special place in Vera's heart. His name was Joe Cadwallader, and he wanted to be a chef but the closest he had come this summer anyway was to work as a dishwasher and a busboy. He slogged around all day in the white waiter's top and cap that they made even the bus-boys wear and gazed longingly at the plates of artistically rendered meals the waiters carried out, hoisted high above their shoulders on one hand.

"It's not right," Joe said, sucking in air as he passed a joint to Vera who lay beside him on the dock to the girls' cabin.

She and Joe had met one afternoon when he was picking up trays from the guests' rooms. He had caught her holding up a pretty polka dot halter top and looking at herself in the mirror.

"Hello," he knocked on the door, "I'm here for trays."

Vera dropped the blouse on the floor. "I wasn't going to take it," she exclaimed, guiltily.

"Did I say you were going to take it?" he asked.

"No," she replied, bending over to pick up the blouse, fold it, and put it back in the drawer. Then, she made her way efficiently over to the double bed by the window where she began to strip the sheets, pillowcases, and coverlet, preparing to put a new set on.

Joe just stood looking at her with a big grin on his face. "Maybe you should have. Taken it. It would look good on you. But then, any-thing would look good on you."

Vera shook out the bottom sheet and tucked it in, military style, at the corners, as she had been taught. "Don't you have trays to collect?" she asked without looking up, though secretly she hoped that this boy with his curly Art Garfunkel hair and infectious smile would stay longer and brighten her day.

"Yeah, I guess I'd better get back. I'm Joe, by the way, Joe Cadwallader. I work in the kitchen. Come by and see me some time," he said, tilting his head and smiling.

Vera found herself tilting her head back and smiling in return. "Maybe I will, Joe. Oh, and I'm Vera. Vera Book."

For a couple of weeks, that's all it was with Vera and Joe. They'd see each other as Vera and Violet passed through the main building to pick up their assignments or refresh their supplies, and Joe would tilt his head to the side and smile. Vera would tilt her head in return and grin the biggest grin.

"What are you doing?" Violet asked her. "What's with the head thing and who is that guy anyway? He's got to be twice your age."

"He's not twice my age," Vera exclaimed.

"No? Well how old is he? Old enough to make it statutory rape."

"Violet. Don't be gross. We're just flirting."

"Well, stop it. It looks ridiculous, rotating your head like you're an emu or something," asserted Violet, who had become more out-spoken since shedding 25 pounds.

"Tilting. We just tilt it to the side a little bit like this and grin." Vera demonstrated the motion to her sister, at which point Violet shoved her gently, laughing.

"Why don't you just sleep with the guy already?"

"But you said statutory rape …."

"I was just kidding. He can't be more than 17."

"He's 21," Vera said quietly.

Vera and Violet lugged their buckets, mops, and vacuum cleaner upstairs, walking in silence down the heavily carpeted hall. "Do Not Disturb" flags decorated the hallway and the girls wondered if they would ever get out for the day.

At the first free room, Vera turned to Violet.

"Do you really think I should lose my virginity with him?" Vera asked. Her sister smiled a laughing smile that lit up her face with a rosy glow.

"You didn't," Vera said aghast.

"No. Not with Joe," Violet quickly explained.

"With whom then?" Vera probed.

"I can't tell you."

"Why not?" Vera asked.

"You'll be mad."

"No, I won't," Vera insisted.

"You promise?"

"Violet!"

"All right. With Brad."

"The life guard boy?"

Violet nodded her head quickly. Vera wondered many things, like how the life guard boy who had referred to Violet as "the Beast" suddenly had a change of heart. Unless he hadn't had a change of heart and he was just being mean and ugly. In which case, she would kill him. But Violet seemed so pleased with herself, prettier, lighter. Maybe this was good for her. Vera wondered how he was in bed, and if they had used protection, and if Violet had stupidly gone and fallen in love.

"You haven't fallen in love with him, have you?" Vera asked gently.

"God, no," Violet said, as she plugged the vacuum into the wall socket. "I could never fall in love with someone as shallow as him."

"I have to say, Violet, you are really surprising me," Vera admitted, as she carried a bucket of cleaners into the bathroom.

Violet giggled. "I know! Right? I'm surprising myself. I feel like a new person. This has been the best summer ever!"

That is how Vera ended up in bed with Joe.

ꙮ

It all started with ice cream. One afternoon as Vera was scrubbing out a particularly nasty toilet and regretting the day she had let her mother talk her into this Godforsaken job, Joe stuck his head in the doorway, knocking on the frame.

"Hey!" he said.

"Hey," Vera responded, wiping loose strands of hair out of her eyes with her rubber gloved arm.

"Want to go for ice cream tonight?" he asked.

"Love to," she replied without hesitation.

"Great. I'll be done around 9:00. Meet you at the red chairs." Then, he disappeared as fast as he had come.

Vera stopped her cleaning for a moment and walked across the hall to where Violet was polishing a sink.

"If someone asks you to go out for ice cream, does it really mean ice cream or is it something else?" she asked her sister.

"Hard to tell these days," Violet answered. "Did he say, 'go for ice cream', were those his exact words?"

Vera nodded.

"Then I'd say it's probably safe to assume it's ice cream. Now if he said "Hey (wink wink) want to go (wink wink) for ice cream (wink wink), then I think it would be another story."

Vera was disappointed but not surprised. She was, after all, just seventeen and he was twenty-one. Old enough to be charged with rape if anyone found out. Old enough to go to war.

"Why didn't you go to Vietnam?" Vera asked him later as she licked her mint chocolate chip cone, her favorite flavor.

"Lucky," he replied. "My number was high. Not true for a lot of friends of mine." Suddenly, he was sullen. He rose and walked over to the metal trash bin and threw his cone away. Vera wanted to ask what was wrong, what he was thinking about, but she already knew. She rose and walked to the metal bin and threw her cone away too. Then, she stood in front of him and waited for a long time as he held his head in his hands, elbows propped on his knees.

Finally, she spoke. "I should go home."

"No," he said, reaching up for her with one hand. "Don't leave me."

She took his hand in her own and sat down on the bench beside him. It was a cool evening and late, but neither of them had to work in the morning, so she gave herself permission just to sit and watch the trickle of late night customers flow into the bright ice-cream stand with its giant plastic soft serve cone on its roof, until the last customer came and went and the lights of the stand were extinguished and it was very dark and quiet.

"I'd better get home," Vera said again, thinking of Violet and their morning swim, but wanting this night never to end.

"Don't go. Come back to my room with me. Let's get high," Joe said.

Vera, who had never been high because of the promise she made to Vern because Veronica was hooked on cocaine, would have preferred alcohol. Something like a good stiff gin and tonic or a bottle of rich red wine, but she had promised Violet that she wouldn't drink and that was a promise she wanted to keep. Vern? He was far away and he'd never know. She made up her mind.

"Sure. Let's go."

Getting high wasn't all that Vera had imagined it would be. First, there was the smoking and inhaling that conjured up bad memories of Valley, and a series of Valley memories followed: Valley burning a hole in Vera's favorite, and only, new white coat; Valley reeking of smoke and cigarettes; Valley crashing the car. But soon, the pot kicked in and Vera was feeling warmer, fuzzier, sillier, lightheaded, not the way that she felt when she drank. Just the opposite: happy, beautiful, and sexy.

The sexy part she really began to feel when Joe turned on the "Moody Blues" and motioned for her to lie down in the bed beside him. Something about the plaintive music and Joe kissing her neck, and licking her wrists and the insides of her arms, and pressing his eager lips to hers made her more excited and sensitive than she had ever felt before. When the song belted out "I love, love you!" she felt that she would burst. This was the feeling that she had waited for, a feeling of climbing out of her own soul into someone else's heart, and feeling attached, molded, connected, one. And they weren't even having sex yet, she thought, only they were. This was sex. This was what sex was, a release from self. Sex, drugs, and rock and roll. She got it. This was the ultimate trip.

When Joe pulled off her shorts and panties, so gently, and she felt his stiff penis against her leg, she knew that this was it. The moment she had wondered about all her life, the instance in which she would lose her virginity. She should be sick with anticipation or scared out of her mind, she thought, but she wasn't. The pot took care of that. She felt some pressure, a little cramping, and then done. He was in her, dancing, and she was dancing too. She was no longer just one of Vern's daughters or another chapter in Valley's book. She was a woman.

The following morning when she turned the key in the lock to their little cabin and found Violet sleeping with Glorioso at her side, Vera felt a little sad. Something so monumental had taken just an instant and with a man she didn't really know. She wondered for a moment if all life's great occasions—births, weddings, funerals, graduations—were just blips on the radar. Losing her virginity seemed so inconsequential, so unmemorable. The really big things that marked you forever were the unkind word tossed out in a heated conversation or promises broken and forgotten, or even love, freely given as you stand at the end of a dock in Minnesota hugging a sister who understands the loneliness you feel, that even a night of sex cannot take away.

NEW GOALS

IN 1973, RONNIE LEFT NEW YORK CITY AND MOVED TO A HALFWAY house, a place where addicts in recovery can stay while they're getting their lives together, in Vermont. To the postman, the house was just known as 1787 Route 313, but to those who lived there, the old farmhouse with its stone walls and orchard was known as "Serenity Place." In the rear of the house, nestled in a grove of pine trees that extended to the perimeter of the acreage, were three compact cottages, affectionately called Happy, Joyous, and Free. There the residents resided, men in one building, women in the next, and staff in the third. Not far from the buildings, and under the shade of the trees, were several picnic tables, and seated at one was Ronnie. She drank a cup of coffee as she listened to the white-haired man across the table from her talk quietly, passing papers to her as he spoke, his thick white moustache muffling his words. Then, he rose and left her at the picnic table in the sun.

He wanted her to write about goals. "We can't in good conscience let you leave here without a plan in mind," he had said, gently. "What is it you want to do next?"

Next, Ronnie thought to herself. She knew what she didn't want to do. She didn't want to do drugs, that was for damned sure. And she didn't want to go back to Iowa and run the farm for Vern either. What she had discovered, when she was at the poets' enclave, was that as much as she really loved writing poetry, it was a personal thing. She didn't want to try to make a living of it. As she wrestled with writing down her goals in life, a requisite part of the counseling she was receiving, she was stumped. She lifted her head up from her paper and put the eraser end of her pencil in her mouth.

Just then, a person appeared at the table. The person was standing with their back against the sun, and as Ronnie looked up, trying to shield her eyes, she couldn't tell if it was male or female.

"Mind if I join you," a most definitely female voice asked. Ronnie put her hand down.

"Of course, it's not my table."

"Does Dr. Dan have you working on goals?" the woman asked.

"Um hum," Ronnie replied.

"Me too. It sucks," she said, to which Ronnie agreed.

"I haven't got a clue what to say. I'm never going to get out of here," Ronnie confessed.

"What did you do before this?" the woman asked, turning her body to face Ronnie's. It was then that Ronnie noticed just how beautiful she was. Tall, with lean limbs defined by her tight, bell bottom pants, and a gorgeous mane of tawny hair, she had eyes like a tiger's, green and gold. Ronnie was stunned and, though she didn't know it yet, fell instantly in love.

"I, eh, I was in vet school. Dropped out," Ronnie said quietly. The woman broke into a wide smile.

"No kidding? Me too!" the stranger cried. "I'm thinking of finishing up my credits at a community college nearby. Then transferring to UVM."

"That sounds like a plan to me," Ronnie smiled.

"You could do it too. I could use the support." The woman gave Ronnie a pleading smile.

Ronnie, ever practical, considered the situation from all sides. What if she did return to school? How would she pay for it? And what then? Where would she practice? With this woman who appeared out of nowhere and seemed to have all the answers for her life? Then again, Ronnie thought, it could be worse. It was, after all, what she wanted but was too stubborn to ask for.

"I'm thinking of going back," Ronnie said.

"Now that sounds like a plan!" the woman said with a twinkle in her eye. Ronnie turned back to the sheets of paper and began scribbling down notes. She didn't know where this was going, but something told her to trust. The woman rose and held out her hand.

"By the way," she said. "I'm Parker. Parker Jones."

UNCONDITIONAL LOVE

THE ONLY BOOK SISTER WHO HAD NO ASPIRATIONS TO GO TO COL-
lege was the lavender-eyed Violet. She had watched her older sisters peel off, one by one, and even her younger sibling, Vera, who
left the house when she was 17. But Violet stayed at home, cooking
and cleaning, helping around the farm and with the "twins," who
were in high school and needed things done—rides, mending, alibis
(for Virginia). Violet was always there. Only she wasn't there. In her
mind she was elsewhere, in another body (hers was still corpulent)
or another time. She imagined that she was Cinderella and her two
younger sisters were the step-sisters, but really, she knew that was
not true. The only person who was ugly to her was Vern. He bad-
gered her, teased her. He humiliated her. Finally, he made her an
offer she couldn't refuse.

"Your Uncle Mike and Aunt Arlene, in Boston, know a family
who is looking for a nanny for their baby girl. You interested?" he
asked. She was.

The family, two college professors on sabbatical at Harvard
from Oxford, England, had a baby girl named Julia. Violet fell in love
with those pink apple cheeks and long, dark eyelashes. So, in 1975,
Violet went to live with the family, doing all that she did at home, plus

minding Julia, for which she was appreciated and paid. Violet didn't care about the money, just watching Julia grow was enough. She saw the baby take her first steps, catching her in Violet's welcoming arms as she stumbled awkwardly across the floor. Violet heard Julia utter her first word, something like "Buh" as they sat quietly watching the birds at the feeder. When Julia wrapped her arms around Violet's thick legs and wouldn't let go, the older girl was smitten.

One day, Violet took Julia to the neighborhood park. It was a beautiful summer day and the park was overflowing with families out to enjoy the day. Violet kept a watchful eye on Julia lest she dash off and get lost in the crowd. She took the toddler's hand and led her to the swings, lifted her up onto one of the baby seats, and buckled her in, then went behind her and gently pushed, and then a little harder as Julia cried "More!" A woman next to Violet who was pushing her own child in a swing, commented, "She's a beauty. She looks just like you."

"Thank you," Violet replied spontaneously. When she realized what she'd done, lied about Julia being her own, she knew that it was time to leave. Not just the park, but the family. Because truthfully all she wanted to do was run away with this baby who had made her into someone that people saw as beautiful, a child who had transformed her with unconditional love.

LIFE CUT SHORT

VIVECA MEANS "LIFE," WHICH IS IRONIC BECAUSE SHE DIED AT SUCH an early age. Twenty. Viveca was a good girl, a Godly girl who hung out at youth group and wore tie-dyed T-shirts with Bible verses stenciled on them. But it wasn't all pretext with Viveca. She didn't spout chapter and verse and then sneak around having sex in the hayloft or slandering other girls who she envied because they were more popular than she was. Viveca was true. She was honest and she was true. She stood out in the corn field with the stalks towering above her and gave herself to God, heart and soul, pleading with him to forgive her family for their sins, to help them see the Light, to redeem them all in the Glory of His name. She felt so blessed, to have this personal relationship with God. It was a Love that filled up her heart, gave her Joy and Hope, made her life bearable and worth living.

She prayed, continuously, while she washed the dishes, seeing every bubble as a little sphere filled with God's love. Against the backdrop of her drunken father shouting obscenities at Valley, who sat immobile in front of the television, watching junk shows, and drinking, too, Viveca prayed that they could be saved. From themselves. From their past. From the world around them. She helped Vern with the farm, feeding the animals and mucking stalls, harvesting vegetables and thanking God for all the blessings in her life. On Sunday, after attending the early service, she volunteered to take care of the babies and toddlers in the nursery for 10 o'clock services. Once a week, she drove all the way into town to the small brick public library and read to the preschoolers, entertaining them with her many voices and expressions as she brought *Chika Chika Boom Boom* and *Where the Wild Things Are* to life. All the while she floated along on her faith waiting for the Great Director in the sky to tell her what she was supposed to do next. She was patient and kind and persevered. At about 19, she developed a little cough, which irritated Vern to no end, but it wouldn't quit and she attributed that to working with kids and the dust in the air. Then, she started to get pains in her chest, but she never let on to Vern because he would just chide her, calling her weak and telling her to haul the heavy bales of hay without complaining. All the while, she had this voice in her head telling her "nurse. nurse," which she understood to be God speaking to her directly and finally coming through with a roadmap for her life.

She enrolled in a nursing program at the local community college, purchased the white nurse's uniform and sturdy white shoes, and prepared herself for Day 1. As she stood in front of the mirror, her long, dark hair tied up in a bun, her skin tan from the summer's work against the white dress, she saw who she would be for the rest of her life and she smiled. Then she coughed, just once, a deep, penetrating, painful cough that pressed on her chest like a cement block and left a splotch of blood on her white shoes. At first, she didn't make the connection, the red with blood. But when she did, she inhaled sharply and held her breath for several moments, reaching out like a dying person for help, hoping that this would all go away. She checked her nose to make sure it wasn't just a nose bleed, but it was not. A trickle of blood ran down the crease from her mouth and she knew this meant business.

Quietly and calmly, without telling anyone, she made an appointment with their family doctor, who saw her and called an oncologist on the spot. "This can't wait," he told Viveca seriously, and she knew she'd have to forgo classes for at least one day. All the while, she tried to be strong, not to think about the future or no future, if that was God's will. She really felt too young to die. She had barely lived. What had she ever done except taken care of the babies at the church and read to the kids in the library and stayed with Valley and Vern when everyone else had baled on them? She wasn't half as selfish as Virginia or as screwed up as Violet or as drunk as Vera. Veronica and Victoria, she barely knew. *Why me, God, why me? What did I ever do to You but love You and serve You and give You my heart?*

Of course, she said to herself as she pulled into the doctor's office, I don't know anything yet. It could be allergies or pneumonia or any number of things. So, she sat on the orange vinyl couch and leafed through *Family Circle* and *Woman's Day* until they finally called her in.

"So, what seems to be the problem?" the serious doctor said as he pressed an icy cold stethoscope against her chest. When she was a nurse, she told herself, she would warm the stethoscope in her hands before putting it against a patient's flesh, and she would never, never look that serious.

"Well, I've had this cough …." she began.

"How long?" he asked.

"Six months. Maybe eight."

"Anything else?"

"Chest pains. Really bad chest pains lately."

"Weight loss?"

"Yeah, but I've been trying."

"Cough up blood?"

"Yes. Yesterday for the first time."

He looked up at her, this time a little kinder, and asked, "Do you smoke?"

"No. But my mom does. Has forever."

"We're going to take some films and then we'll see what we've got. Meanwhile, make yourself comfortable. It shouldn't be too long."

It was long, very long, possibly the longest day that Viveca had ever known. It was a day full of questions and reminiscences and dreams. Regrets over things she had done and said and over things she had not. She wished, of course, that she had been kinder to her sisters. That went without saying. She wished that she had greater faith, that she could truly embrace God's will for her, whatever that was. But more than that, she wished that she had let Matt, one of the local boys who helped Vern from time to time, kiss her and make love to her and get her pregnant. She wished she hadn't been so self-righteous and that she had had kids. The way things were going, she would never have kids. Not even one. And that made her very, very sad. But then, she told herself looking on the bright side, if I had kids, and I died, they wouldn't have a mother, so better not to have had kids at all.

The doctor called her in at about 3:45. He was all cheerfulness and optimism, and Viveca was relieved to know that everything was going to be all right. He chatted with her about her family and how she had spent the summer; she relaxed knowing that this was all a nonissue, that the films had shown nothing, that she was good. Then, as suddenly as he was congenial, he turned serious. Very serious. He slapped the films up onto the lighted board and began circling his hands over large, dark splotches which she could only imagine were her lungs. She was confused, listening but not hearing a word that he said until finally he stopped motioning and looked directly at her. "There is no delicate way to say this, Viveca. You have esophageal cancer and it's pretty far gone. I'll do what I can to make you comfortable. If you have any loose ends, you best tie them up now. I'm sorry."

Viveca sat on her chair, silent, for several minutes. Finally, she spoke. "Do you know what my name means —Viveca?"

"No," he said, quietly.

"It means Life. Either this is somebody's idea of a joke or it's a message from God that I need to fight."

The doctor just smiled.

"I know it's going to be a hard fight," she continued, wiping the tears that had started to trickle from her eyes.

The doctor nodded.

"But I'm going to fight. Will you fight with me?" she asked, earnestly.

"I would if I could," he said as he stood stoically by while she stifled the urge to throw herself into his arms.

Back at the farm, Valley was watching *Let's Make a Deal*, drinking her "before dinner drink." "How was school?" she asked Viveca without looking up. "Did you meet anyone nice?"

"I didn't go," Viveca said quietly.

"What's that? You don't know?" Valley cried.

Viveca walked over to the television set and turned it off. "I said I didn't go!" she exploded.

"What? Why not?" Valley asked, concerned.

"I've spent the day in doctors' offices," she began.

"Are you sick? Is it that little cough?"

"I coughed up blood, Valley."

"Oh dear, that can't be good." Valley said as she started to pull a cigarette out of the pack beside her and light it.

"PUT THAT AWAY!" Viveca screamed.

"Viveca!"

"Valley! I have esophageal cancer. It's inoperable. I'm going to die!"

"No, you're not. No, you're not," Valley repeated as she shoved the cigarette back into the pack. "You don't have cancer. If anyone should have cancer, it should be me."

"But it's not. It's me. Because I grew up around you, and it's killing me. You are killing me, Valley."

Valley took her whiskey glass and threw it straight at Viveca's head only her aim was off and it landed on the television screen, cracking it so that it looked like a spider's web. Viveca stared at her mother, boring holes in her soul, and after several good long minutes, she walked away.

∽

The only place that Viveca wanted to be was with Matt. She didn't want to stand in the cornfields, weeping, lest Vern find her and chastise her for being emotional and weak. She couldn't stay home with Valley who, naturally, made this all about her; she'd wear her guilt and shame like a mantel over her shoulders, wrapping herself in regret until she emerged the victim and everyone crooned "Poor Valley. Poor, poor Valley, what a life you have had to bear." Valley the Victim, when it was her, Viveca, whose life was cut short by years. She couldn't go to church because she was so mad at God right now that she'd spit on him if he came near. What had this all been, some cruel joke, let me get you to love me beyond all else and then watch me hurt you beyond belief? She had grown up with parents like that. She didn't need any more. She was going to go see Matt and let him kiss her with those luscious, plump lips, and look at her naked with his electric blue eyes. She would let him love her, again and again, and when they were done, again. She would be warm in his embrace, nurtured, and for a moment the fear would be gone.

By now the tears were streaming from Viveca's eyes and she was wiping snot from her nose with the back of her arm. She looked in her rear-view mirror and saw that there was a young woman driving with two kids bouncing around in the seats. They all looked like they were singing. Viveca smiled. She remembered the days when she was younger and Valley had been sweet. They took rides to the lake or into the country and they sang Beatles songs all the way there. "It's Been a Hard Day's Night," "Help," and "Yellow Submarine." Those were good days, when they were young. Vern wasn't so far gone with his drinking and Valley hadn't joined him. The world seemed a kinder place, despite the assassinations and the war. It was easier then, lying under the elm tree on a hot summer day and selling lemonade to no one. Because no one ever came by. Except Valley who put nickels in the cup and let them drink the sweet yellow stuff. She really wasn't bad, Valley, she had just gone down the wrong path.

Viveca was on the right path. She asked God to forgive her and made the decision to go to church instead of to Matt's. God was where she really got her comfort, and even as she made the decision she felt His presence, or someone's presence in the car with her. Of course, she saw nothing, but she knew better. And suddenly, coming at her very fast, was a car, a speeding car pointed right at her, out of his lane. And in an instant, she knew what she had to do. To turn away would mean that the speeding silver car would hit the woman and her two children following behind. She made the decision to stay put and to take the impact whatever that meant for her. Life. Death. None of it mattered. She gripped the wheel and shut her eyes, asked God to help her through this and to let all her family know that the last thing that she thought before she died was, "I love you all."

PARTING SHOTS

I T H A D B E E N T H R E E D A Y S S I N C E V I V E C A ' S A C C I D E N T A N D V A L L E Y hadn't moved from the recliner in front of the TV except to make the occasional bathroom trip or to refill her whiskey glass which Vern kept topping off for her. They both sat, numb, watching old westerns and various game shows on the cracked screen, the sound set loud enough to drown out a jet engine, loud enough to keep them from hearing the thoughts that were going on in their heads. How the arrangements were made for the funeral was a mystery. Somehow, all the girls had been notified, a casket chosen and Viveca's outfit laid out for the viewing. Valley and Vern had wanted a closed cas-ket; they couldn't imagine how Viveca could be put back together enough to present to the friends who knew her. But Jack Torrence, the funeral director, had assured them that his people were artists and Viveca's friends and family deserved this last goodbye. Flowers arrived, and cards, and a multitude of casseroles. Later Vera would discover that Mrs. Brown and Miss Aldridge had teamed together with Nolan Shepherd to make the whole thing as easy as possible for the grieving parents who were thinking not of their dead daughter as much as all the mistakes they'd made, dousing their sorrow in more liquor because they really didn't know what else to do.

Victoria arrived from New York with her nine-year-old son, Artie, in tow. Artie, a sweet boy with coffee-colored skin and a big head of black hair, would have liked to have run over and given his grandma and grandpa a kiss. He was darling, a gentle spirit, the opposite of his arrogant father who had long since abandoned Victoria and his son. No love came from there. His mother, filled with regret over having gotten pregnant and not having the funds to travel abroad for an abortion or the nerve to get one with a questionable doctor, held Artie at arm's length, loving him by scolding him, correcting him, slapping him so that he winced whenever she approached, in a moment of tenderness, to give him a hug. All Artie wanted was love, but these grandparents with their drinking and smoking and dull eyes were not what he sought.

What he sought slammed in the front door, swearing, "God, it's hot in here!" and opening the fridge for something cold, and nonalcoholic, to drink. Violet had arrived.

Artie had never met any of his aunts, though he had heard tales of them, tales which were generally laced with resentment, envy, and regret. In his mind, they were all spidery women put together like matchstick dolls with spindly arms and legs, hairy, and concave chests. When Violet entered the room, with her large, soft curves almost touching the door jambs and her plump, apple cheeks and dazzling violet eyes, Artie didn't know what to make of her. He was a little afraid she might try to scoop him up in a kiss, folding him into her corpulent body, the way his father's fat, black women friends did, but instead she crouched down in front of him, teetering a little, and held out her velvet soft hand, taking his small one, shaking it, and saying respectfully, "Artie? I'm your Aunt Violet. It's a pleasure to meet you." Then, she toppled over onto her substantial posterior and laughed uproariously while Artie tried to stifle a smile.

"Oh, c'mon there, darling, you can laugh. It's funny! Your aunt falling on her ass!" she said, winking at him. Thereafter, he stuck to her like glue.

Within the hour, Veronica and Vera had both arrived. Everyone stood around in the living room, sipping on bourbon, except Violet and Artie who found some juice, and watching Valley and Vern watching their shows and ignoring the fact that their offspring had congregated in the room around them for the first time in a decade.

"Does anyone know what time we're supposed to go over," Violet whispered to Ronnie, who always took charge and had ever since she was a child.

"Now," Ronnie responded. "We should be going now."

"What about Virginia?" Violet asked.

"She'll get here when she gets here. We can't wait any longer," Ronnie stated simply.

Then, turning to Valley and Vern, she said, "C'mon Valley and Vern. You can ride with me."

The funeral home was located in an old house near the center of town. From the outside, it looked pleasant enough with its fresh white paint, shiny black shutters, and red metal roof glistening in the sun. Inside it smelled of old age and sadness which seeped from the stale green walls and up from the worn black floral carpeting. Valley gave one huge sigh when she entered the building and clutched Ronnie's hand.

In the main room, lying in a cherry wood casket on white silk sheets that puffed up around her like a cloud, was Viveca. The "artist" at the funeral home had, indeed, done a spectacular job. There were no traces of trauma or distress on her that Vera could see. She had never looked more innocent or radiant than she did in death. Vera thought that she looked like some pre-Raphaelite painting, a beautiful girl with alabaster skin and plum-colored lips, long dark hair curling around her face and breasts. A single white rose held in her right hand and a golden cross on a chain in the left.

"She looks like Snow White," Violet whispered as she stood looking down on her dead sister. "Only I guess she's not going to wake up."

Valley exploded with grief, as did Violet then, who put her arms around her mother and let her weep. Ronnie gazed stoically at her baby sister, thinking to herself that it was a damned shame that such a lovely creature had been taken from Earth so soon. Victoria calculated the cost of the casket, the embalming, the flowers, and the funeral, and wondered how Valley and Vern would be able to pay. She hoped they wouldn't turn to her for help, she being the oldest and all. But she was on a limited budget, playing gigs at piano bars and sharing, as she and Artie did, a single room in a boarding house. If her parents asked, she would spread the costs evenly among the five remaining girls. Vern was numb, deadened by the turn of events that had led him to this point in his life. All his good intentions had amassed to create this shit pile. He didn't know how it could get any worse.

Just then, a resilient voice from the back of the room called out, "There you are! You have no idea how much trouble I have had finding this place." An orange-haired woman strode up the room toward the casket carrying a Walkman and wearing a skimpy black mini dress and high, high heels, slinging a dead fox stole over her left shoulder which she held carefully with her right hand, flashing a huge diamond ring that she intended for everyone to comment on. She looked familiar, but no one could quite place her. She looked like a movie star, with traces of Virginia still in her face. Then giggling, "Oh c'mon guys, it's me Ginger! Virginia!" she air kissed her father and mother, wriggling her way up to the casket, and looking down on her "twin," though they could barely be called twins now. While Viveca's beauty seemed totally natural, and spirituality oozed from every pore, Virginia had become a material girl. Recent surgery had enhanced her breasts and her lips, which protruded like platters in the lips of Ubangi women in Africa. Her fake tan skin was the color of a pumpkin or a tangerine. Her hair, once a comfortable brown, was now the bright orange of a summer peach, stiff from product, and teasing and sticky to the touch. All Virginia ever wanted to be was the most beautiful Book sister. And rich. But now, staring at her little sister, she thought she could never compete with death. People would forever remember Viveca as this ethereal angel, exquisite beyond words. Forever young. Virginia consoled herself with the next thought which was, "Forever dead." The joke is on you, Virginia said silently to her sister. "You may be the bride of Jesus, but I've got this," she whispered, laying her right hand on Viveca's chest, which everyone around her took to be a motion of endearment but which Virginia meant to rub in that she was alive to spend money. "That's for ratting me out to Dad that time I was smoking in the barn and getting me put in the root cellar overnight," she whispered into her sister's ear, then turned on her considerably high heels and walked over to sit by herself, brooding.

Once the family finished paying their respects, the doors were opened to the public. A line quickly formed that snaked around from the receiving line, through the chapel, and out into the parking lot. Valley was amazed at the outpouring for her family, and she met the mourners with phrases that eventually became cliché. "She looks beautiful, as always," they would say, and she would reply, "Yes she does, doesn't she?" Or "She was a truly exceptional young woman," which Valley would acknowledge with, "Yes, she was, wasn't she?" "We're going to miss her." "Yes, we will, won't we?" Valley mouthed these words repeatedly until her lips grew as numb as the feelings inside. No child should die before a parent, she told herself. But hers had. Viveca's death was the thick, iron door that would shut Valley finally into her self-imposed prison. From now until her death, she would torture herself with self-doubt and blame so that relationships with those around her became impossible. Her health would dwindle. Her interests waned, until there was nothing left but the memory of Viveca shouting at her, "You killed me, Valley!" And still, she couldn't quit the cigarettes, though she tried many times, and each time she lit up she felt nothing but disgust for herself and fury at the God who had taken her beautiful young daughter instead of her.

Vern, meanwhile, reeking of alcohol, grew more and more agitated as the line seemed not to lessen but increase. While a part of him was moved by this outpouring of support, a greater part needed a cigarette and a drink. And he wasn't even a smoker. Time and again, he ran his index finger around his collar and mopped his sweating forehead with the old handkerchief Victoria had insisted that he bring. Finally, he could bear it no longer and he bolted from the line and headed for the side door.

"Where are you going, Vern?" Vera said as she laid her hand on his arm and stopped him in his tracks.

"I need some air," he said, shaking her off, and leaving.

She watched him go, filled with embarrassment and regret that even in this instance he couldn't behave like a gentleman. But she knew. She knew that what he needed was a stiff belt or two to get him through, to quell the tremors in his hands. She felt the same way. She'd love to join him in the back lot taking hits off a pint, but she couldn't because she needed to set an example and put on the gracious face of one who mourns, but who is grateful, for all the world to see so that someone, many some ones, would leave the visitation not thinking how crude the Books were, but rather how elegant and serene they were in their grief, rather like princesses with impeccable manners.

"Hi. I'm Matt Stanfield," said the young man holding out his hand to Vera. "I am a friend of Viveca."

"Thank you, Matt, for coming. It means a lot …." Vera began.

"Actually, I was more than a friend. I loved her. Was in love with her. We would have been married …." he said as he broke down in tears.

Vera was floored, ambushed by her own emotions which caused tears to pinch at her eyes and heat to swell in her cheeks. She hadn't really ever thought of Viveca as girlfriend material, sexual in any way. She was more like a saint, a chaste virgin. But here was this handsome boy with closely cropped blonde hair and Caribbean blue eyes who was saying he loved her! Suddenly, it all became real. Viveca was not a saint waiting to ascend into the arms of Jesus! How cruelly they all had mocked her, made assumptions about her that were not just. In reality, she was a healthy, lusty young woman who loved this gorgeous boy. Suddenly, her death seemed such a waste, a tragedy.

"They say she saved that family," he continued.

Vera nodded, holding her index finger under her nose to keep back the tears.

"She was so good. I'll never find anyone …."

"Come. Come with me," Vera said, taking his hand and leading him over to the casket. She marched deliberately, sure that she was breaking protocol, but certain that Viveca would have wanted it this way. When they stood at the casket, she reached in and unwrapped the gold cross and chain that was wound around Viveca's left hand. Then, she took Matt's hand, put them in it, and curled his fingers over them.

"I can't. Won't your Mom …." he began.

"My Mom doesn't give a rat's ass about this. I am certain that of all the people in the world Viveca would have wanted to have these, it would be you."

Matt folded Vera in a hefty embrace, whispering, "Thank you. I loved her so much." And Vera whispered back, "Thank you."

Back outside, Ronnie sat with Vern. They were silent, sitting in the hot September sun. Vern had taken off his jacket and laid it on the hood of a stranger's car. He drank, in small sips, with the movement of a rocking chair: to his lips, away from his lips, to his lips away from his lips. Intermittently, he wiped tears from his eyes.

"She wasn't my favorite," he began. "You were always my favorite, Ronnie. But she was special. She was the last. She was my baby, my final hope. When she turned to Jesus, I didn't have much to say to her. Truth is, I thought she was a damned fool, snookered into that religion thing. But I guess she did a lot of good with them babies and all. She never bothered your mother and me. Always kept everything clean. Did her own laundry, cooked, and helped with chores. I see now I'd gotten used to it, taken it for granted. I shouldn't have taken her for granted. Valley was so mad at her that night, so I got mad too, protecting Valley. If I had just stopped her from driving away ....." He stopped in the middle of his sentence and dropped his head into both hands, then sat upright and swigged again.

"You can't blame yourself, Vern," Ronnie offered.

Vern looked at her with angry, righteous eyes. "I can blame myself. I can and I will. For the rest of my life I will blame myself that my baby is dead."

The rest of the evening was subdued. The girls found themselves in their old beds and everyone slept fitfully only to rise in the dark for the burial which was to take place at sunrise, the one request that Viveca had made to Valley as they drove to church one Easter morning for a sunrise service. "When I die," she had said, "I'd like to be buried at sunrise so my soul can rise up with the sun's rays." "Really?" Valley had asked. Valley took that to mean that Viveca was playing with homonyms, sun and son, as she was so preoccupied with the Son of God, there's no telling what she would do.

At the cemetery, the cluster of Books stood rigidly attentive as Viveca's casket was removed from the hearse. Violet and Vera were weeping, as were Valley and Ronnie, who wiped away tears from her eyes. Victoria held onto Artie like a shield, her placid face masking the inner turmoil she felt inside. It was only Virginia who seemed unmoved and was actually more concerned with when she'd get her next smoke than her "twin" who was being borne on the shoulders of the pallbearers. Six men, including Matt Stanfield and Nolan Shepherd, carried the casket. The others, two boys and two men, Valley, who was hiding behind a pair of enormous Jackie O sunglasses, recognized from church. Vern stumbled after the casket, raising his arms, whether to help or in supplication was not clear. He shuffled along, crying and lurching, still drunk from the night before, until he finally fell to his knees, put his hands over his face, and wept. The girls watched their father, some with charity others with disgust. No one was quite as embarrassed as Victoria who saw her father for the pathetic case that he had become. As Vera would tell her many years later, "It takes one to know one."

When they stood at the graveside solemnly listening to the minister echo a few prayers and deliver the rites of passage, Matt Stanfield slipped away and then returned with a boom box which he set down on the ground in front of him. Just as the minister was intoning "ashes to ashes, dust to dust," Matt called out, "Wait. We aren't done." And as the sun rose over the horizon, sending out a glorious golden sheen, he pressed the button and the Beatles' "Here Comes the Sun" began to play. He played it all the way through and then the casket was covered with handfuls of the rich soil that grew the delicious corn in the tall cornfields where Viveca had had secret conversations with God. "Here I am God. Take me. I'm yours." And He did.

Back at the house, all hell broke loose. Victoria stood in the kitchen with Valley and Vern, surrounded by a sea of casseroles and cold salads that covered the countertops and table. Kind neighbors and churchgoers had tentatively approached the front door when they heard the shouting, shoved the food into the younger girls' waiting hands, and run nervously away lest something explode. In fact, Victoria was having a meltdown. After six shots of whiskey, and as many beers, her self-righteousness and "honesty" levels were well lubricated.

"How dare you," she began, pointing an accusing finger at Vern, "show up drunk to your own daughter's funeral? How can you possibly think that would be a good thing?!"

When Vern just stood there sipping on his liquor, Victoria reached into the cupboard, pulled out several ceramic dinner plates and smashed them all to the floor. Violet's hand leapt to her mouth, while Virginia turned away stifling a laugh.

"Smashed? You want to see smashed. I'll show you smashed (crash) and shitfaced (crash) and hammered (crash) and sloshed (crash.) What I can't show you is a father who cares enough about her baby girl not to get DRUNK the day of her funeral!!!"

"Victoria!" Valley, herself drunk and yelling, interrupted the tirade. "That's enough. Your father is coping with this the best that he can."

"Bullshit!" Victoria yelled. "He's coping with this like he copes with everything. He's drunk. He's just a drunk."

A whiskey glass sailed past Victoria's ear, just nicking it enough to send a hot flash through the girl's brain.

"You didn't just throw that at me. You did throw that at me? You could have killed me! Isn't one dead daughter enough for you? C'mon Artie. Artie? We are getting out of this asylum now," Victoria said as she turned on her heels and marched off to find her son.

He was on the front porch with Violet, swinging on the porch swing. Violet had her hands over Artie's ears and was speaking to him in low, soothing tones about how everything was going to be alright. Artie's eyes were closed and he was clutching Violet's hands. He had been crying. They rocked in the swing, enjoying the gentle breeze accompanied by the scratchy squeak of the chair, keeping the world at bay.

"C'mon Artie, we're leaving." Immediately he dropped down out of the swing, reached up to give Violet a hug, turned one last time with a wave, and then they were gone.

The other girls were scattered throughout the house. Ronnie was in the kitchen sweeping up the broken dishes and glass as Valley and Vern sat, per instruction, with their feet up off the floor to avoid shards. Ronnie had no opinion on what had just happened, though Valley and Vern were egging her on to take sides.

"It's not my fault she drove off that night," Vern whined.

"He was only protecting me. Viveca was so mad," Valley chimed in.

"Valley didn't mean to throw that glass. She'd been drinking too much," Vern spewed the awful truth.

Precisely, thought Ronnie as she swept, wishing she could sweep time away the way she could sweep the broken glass. But life just is what it is.

"What did you say, Veronica?" Valley asked.

"Nothing," she replied.

"But I heard you. You said something," Valley insisted.

Ronnie stopped sweeping and stood tall, holding the broom with both hands. "I said 'life is what it is.' And so is death. There's no going back."

"Yes," said Valley," but how do I go forward from here?"

"That, Mom, is the million-dollar question. How DO you go forward from here?" Ronnie said and resumed her sweeping until she was convinced the way was clear.

Virginia had been looking for a place to steal a smoke. She had cloistered herself in the upstairs bathroom where she kneeled on the closed toilet seat and blew smoke out of the hexagonal window which she had pried open with a nail file from her purse. Someone had done a piss-poor job of painting this, she thought as she hacked away until the window finally popped loose. She wished that she was back in Dallas where everyone was impressed with her lips, her boobs, and her ring. Back to where people understood her and appreciated her desire to make something more of herself, to lift herself into a higher echelon of existence where people cared about appearances and things and power. Far away from her drunk Mama and Papa and her sisters who would now look at her as the baby when, really, wasn't she acting just a little bit more mature than they were? She certainly had more money than any of them, and that had to count for something. Telling herself that, feeling better about herself, she was ready to face the family again. She took one final drag on her cigarette, dropped the butt into the toilet and flushed, and exhaled deeply once more out the small portal. Then, she headed down the hall toward the stairs, which is when she saw Vera sitting on the bed in Viveca's room.

Vera sat in the emptiness and quiet of her dead sister's room. After a few moments, she rose and gently opened Viveca's top drawer, inside which were, neatly folded, a dozen pairs of white underwear and several small, delicate white bras with a single rosebud at the cleavage, and white socks that were balled into fists. Vera closed the drawer and looked around at the walls which were painted Virgin Blue. The walls were mostly bare, except for several pieces of art-work: a hand painted plaque that read "It is well with my soul" and a flowery reproduction of the 23rd psalm. There was a small, wooden crucifix at the head of her bed and, incongruously, the Beatles' *Abbey Road* poster on the opposite wall.

The room, other than the Beatles' poster, resembled a nun's cell in a convent. Simple, peaceful, and clean. Vera walked over to the window, looking out at the acres of corn that begged to be harvested, to the red barn and the pasture by the barn where Miss Maybelline and Blessing shoveled the dirt for some grass. Then, suddenly, some-thing crashed into the window and Vera jumped, stifling a scream. Looking down, she saw on the porch roof below her the shuddering corpse of a small bird, taking its last breath. Nothing could keep back Vera's tears and she cried not just for Viveca, whose life was cut too short, too soon, and not just for her family that seemed so hell-bent on destruction, but for herself as she felt herself falling down a slip-pery slope toward her own demise, and she was frightened and angry at the same time. She wanted to live. She had promise. She believed in her future but she just didn't know how to get there. So she did the only thing she could think of as she wept in Viveca's room. She fell to her knees, shut her eyes, clasped her hands together, and said from the bottom of her heart, "Help me."

She didn't know who she was talking to, maybe Viveca, now with the angels, maybe simply the air, but she knew as soon as the words flew from her lips that something powerful had happened.

She didn't know when, she didn't know where or how, but she knew that help was on its way. With that, she rose and walked down the stairs, passing Virginia who was standing in the shadows.

"What do you want?" Vera asked her younger sister.

Virginia shook her head vigorously. "Nothing," she said.

"Don't lie, Virginia. It's not attractive," Vera advised as she walked down the stairs, grabbed her coat and bag, and began to walk out to her car to begin the long journey back to Boston. But something stopped her, prompted her to go into the kitchen, and kiss everyone goodbye. She wished she could say she felt love for them all, but really, all she felt was hollow. Still, better a hollow hug than no hug at all. Better to feign affection than to throw plates and yell slurs and have to clean up all that mess after. Or was it? She really didn't know.

As she climbed into her beige VW Bug and drove away, she had this awful, awesome feeling that things would never be the same.

IN THE END IS MY BEGINNING

VERA WOULDN'T HAVE CHANGED A THING ABOUT HER LIFE. NOT the night when she stopped over at a Hampton Inn somewhere in Pennsylvania on the way back from Viveca's funeral, and made her way to the bar, only to get shitfaced and end up skinny dipping with some rosy-cheeked market analyst who she later had sex with, though she couldn't remember his name. Not the champagne parties thrown by the University Press, where she had worked as an intern, an associate editor and now editor since she was 18, for famous authors who, inevitably, sometimes one, sometimes two, ended up in her bed. Not the sick feeling that she got when she woke with a mouth that burned like razors and sand to an anonymous note on her pillow thanking her for the great night, inviting her to Scranton or Dobbs Ferry or Atlanta whenever she was in town. Vera would hold on to those awful feelings of shame, remorse, and regret like precious jewels because they reminded her of who she had been and where she could so easily go again, back to being the girl who hid in the kitchen doing dishes because she was so afraid of taking that first drink, afraid of where it would take her and who she would become. At the end, she was too afraid to drink and too afraid not to. She had caught her father's disease and she knew no cure.

But things began to change. A message emerged on the game board that Vanna White stood by: *Help is on the way.* At first, she brushed it off as coincidence, but when her boss invited her to travel out to California for a trade show, a convention of publishing houses where the University Press would be showcasing its most recent publications, stating, "This should be good for you out there," she was reminded for a flash of her first visit with Kennett Jenkins nearly twenty years before and how she felt that something good was going to come. And it had, it did. He had helped her publish some of her stories when she was a young girl. At 11 years old, she had seen promise for her future, but then she began drinking, Kennett died, and the momentum was lost.

She wasn't that old, only twenty-four, but she felt older than time. She was bone weary. The years since leaving home, when she graduated at seventeen and accepted a full scholarship at a college outside Boston, had been years of fear and anxiety, sex and drugs, and danger and regret. She was tired, very tired and she needed a way out. So when her boss mentioned California, she leapt at the opportunity.

The trade show, held in a monstrous arena somewhere just outside of LA, was uneventful. Crowds of people leafing through books that they weren't really interested in and would probably never read, to ascertain when the famous authors the Press published, specifically Jimmy Carter, were due to arrive for signings.

One of the people who came over to their booth was a young man, in his thirties, himself from California, blonde, with a surfer's tan and build, and eyes as bright blue as the California sky on a smog-free day. His name was Trace Sunday and he sold books. He reminded Vera of Joe Cadwallader, but in a different palette, all smiles and white teeth, exuding testosterone, which was probably why she found herself opening up to an otherwise perfect stranger. She was drawn to him immediately and made a plan to get him into bed, but he was a slow mover, all respectful cordiality and with an educated interest in the titles on the table. Then, he popped the million-dollar question: "Do you write?" he asked her earnestly, a question which took her by surprise and left her speechless. "I only ask because usually when someone works for a publisher, they're a closet writer on the side."

Vera didn't know how to answer. She considered herself a writer, had published a number of short stories and poems, several years ago, albeit in small publications. As a teenager, she had thought that she would be the next great thing on the American literary scene, but now the most she wrote were birthday greetings and sympathy cards. She had helped with Viveca's obituary, but that could hardly count. What had happened? What had gotten in the way? Life? Responsibilities? Growing up? She honestly couldn't blame it on the booze. The booze was what had given her courage to start a new story or to jot down notes on a cocktail napkin for the novel she meant to write. But somehow, the notes smeared and she never moved beyond the inertia, the paralysis that kept her from going forward. She was too afraid not to be a success to risk being a failure, if that made any sense.

"That's an awfully pregnant pause for a 'yes' or 'no' answer," Trace said, interrupting her thoughts.

"Yes, I am—was—an author. A long time ago," she replied.

"Once a writer, always a writer, that's what I say," he replied, congenially. "Like they say, once you're a pickle, you can never go back to being a cucumber."

"Who says that and how does it apply?" she asked, confused.

"Just some friends. Say, would you like to go to dinner tonight. We can talk about how you're not a writer anymore."

"Very funny," she replied, not knowing whether to be irritated or elevated by his perky countenance and his upbeat joie de vivre.

"I'll take that as a 'yes,'" he winked at her. "How's 6:00? I'm an early eater. The restaurant downstairs."

Vera nodded, not really knowing what else to do. Six o'clock was perfect. She would meet him, eat with him, and entice him away to her bed where they would enjoy a night of wild sex. Maybe she should chill a bottle of champagne? Or two? Or was he more of a hard liquor type of guy, Hemingway meets Leo Carrillo State Beach. She thought not. She'd go with the bubbly, like his personality, and see where it led.

When Vera walked into the hotel's restaurant at 6:10, no point in being on time, she thought to herself, better to fabricate a little mystery, she was glad that she had chosen to wear her periwinkle, sleeveless A-line dress and pearls, although she had thought that she might be too overdressed. She was not. Trace stood and greeted her, decked out in white linen trousers, a blush colored shirt open at the neck, and a navy blazer. Beside him was a huge bouquet of exquisite flowers. She thought for a moment that maybe he was gay, but when he scrutinized her up and down, from strappy sandals to gentle curls, she knew that he was not and she breathed a sigh of relief. Not that she had anything against gays; that just wasn't on tonight's agenda.

The first thing Trace did after tucking her into the table and kissing her on the cheek was to turn his wine glass over. Immediate questions rose in Vera's head. Why doesn't he want wine? Doesn't he drink? If he doesn't drink, what does he want with me? Should I leave? The doubt fairies circled her mind like vultures and finally, in a fit of desperation, she turned her wine glass over too, and immediately regretted doing so.

The rest of the dinner was a blur. She had no recollection of what she had said, done, or agreed to do because she had been consumed with thoughts about the booze. How she wasn't having any, how she wanted it, how she couldn't wait to shake hands at the door to her room and dive into the two bottles of champagne she had chilling on ice in the bathroom sink. She could see them there, taste them. She wanted them more than she wanted him, and she knew that was wrong.

"Something the matter?" Trace asked.

"No. Everything's delicious," Vera responded with a broad smile. "It's just that, I was wondering," she continued, gathering all the courage she could muster to go on. "I was wondering why you don't drink. Is it a religious thing or health issues? Are you in training?"

Trace threw back his head and laughed. "Not religious at all, and I'm definitely not in training. Health, you could say yes. I'm allergic to alcohol. When I use it, I break out in asshole."

"What do you mean?" Vera asked, not sure why she was going down this path.

"I have a personality change. I become someone I'm not. I do things I'm not proud of …." he said, quietly.

"Doesn't everyone do that when they drink? Isn't that the whole point?" Vera asked, confused and defensive.

"I don't know about everyone, but I know when I start drinking I can't stop and that doesn't work for me," Trace commented, just a little defensively.

Vera felt a dull, heavy drop in her stomach, but then she cheered herself up, reminding herself that she had stopped many times, and often for quite a while. It was just that lately, she'd been under a lot of stress and stopping didn't seem like an option. She decided that Trace was a very unfortunate man and that she should probably avoid him. But she was too attracted to him to do that just yet.

"Could you have just a little champagne? To celebrate our new friendship?" she asked, coyly.

"Not a drop," he replied.

Vera had had enough. She rose and held out her hand to Trace.

"This has been lovely," she lied, "but I am really exhausted and I have an early morning. Thanks for dinner."

Trace looked at her with an intensity she couldn't name, but it was as though he was peeling her like a banana and reading what was inside the skin. She was sure he knew what she was up to, but she didn't care. So what if she was going upstairs to her room to have a few drinks? It was none of his business anyway. Except that she would have liked to have fallen asleep next to him. But you can't have everything.

"May I walk you up?" he asked, politely.

"No. That's ok. I'm good," Vera said as she reached for her flowers. "Can't forget these!" she laughed.

Trace laid his hand on top of hers and looked her in the eyes. "Be careful, Vera," he said quietly.

"Always," she replied and walked off slowly until she was out of his eyesight, and then she slipped off her shoes and ran to the elevator and leaned against the cool, paneled walls. "Always."

The next morning, or was it noon, Vera was woken by a persistent tapping on her hotel room door. At first, she thought it was the water pipes or maybe a workman somewhere far off, the sound so rhythmic and insistent that it made her already throbbing head pound all the more. But then she heard someone calling her name. "Vera? Vera are you there?" the words swam at her through the muddied waters in her mind.

She rose, holding the side of her head that hurt the most. Went to the door, unlocked it and there was Trace Sunday looking all perky and showered in his chinos and pressed white shirt, sleeves rolled, sporting a tangerine colored tie. Vera was painfully aware that she was wearing the same clothes she had had on the night before when she left him in the restaurant. Her hair was a tangled mess, her mascara had bled in streaks down her cheeks making her look like a harlequin, and her breath felt and tasted like yesterday's garbage. How could she let him in? She started to close the door.

"Mind if I come in?" he asked, so nicely, and with such pleading eyes that she couldn't say no.

Vera snorted and walked away from the door, back to the sofa where she had spent the night. At her feet were two empty bottles of champagne and a sprinkling of empty nips from the mini bar.

"Little party?" he asked, feigning humor. Vera just put her elbows on her knees and held her head in her hands. "You know it's not normal to drink two bottles of champagne and whiskey nips alone in your hotel room."

"Well, you wouldn't join me," she spat out viciously.

"You know I couldn't. And you know why, don't you? You know that I am an alcoholic, a recovering alcoholic."

Actually, Vera knew nothing of the sort. She knew that he chose not to drink but she didn't know why. But him, an alcoholic? He was too cute, clean, polite and young to be an alcoholic. Alcoholics were old wrinkled men, desperate, like her dad.

"Seven years sober," he continued. "I know, I'm too young, right? I was probably about your age when I cleaned up."

Vera was filled with fear and hope at the same time. She desperately wanted to find a way out of the blackness that she was living in, and she knew, with the little bit of honesty she could muster, that booze was the problem, but could she really just give it up? She had tried so often and failed so many times, she didn't think she could take another failure. This stranger gave her hope, so she resigned herself with a sigh.

"I've tried to stay sober. I can't do it," she told him.

"Have you been trying to do it on your own?" he asked.

Of course, she said to herself, what other way is there?

"Would you be willing to try something with me?" At these words, Vera came to attention. She'd be willing to try almost anything with him. "I want you to come with me to a meeting," he said, bending down to look her squarely in the eyes.

"A meeting? What kind of meeting?" she asked, disappointed by his request.

"An Alcoholics Anonymous (AA) meeting." Not knowing anything about AA except that it was for old men in black raincoats, like the CIA, and they travelled in two's, like Jehovah's Witnesses, she wanted to bolt, but she agreed, on one condition. "I'll go to a meeting with you if you'll sleep with me."

"Deal," Trace agreed, knowing full well that he wouldn't until she had a year of sobriety and was well established in the AA program. Years later, Vera reflected on that first AA meeting with Trace. She had felt the outsider as everyone kept greeting Trace and hugging one another. The noise level was acute, but she felt like she was in a bubble. Alone, until a rather ordinary looking woman walked over to her and stuck out her hand.

"I'm Susan," she said. "Are you new?" After that, she could listen, though she didn't hear much, just everyone saying "Hi, so-and-so" after every person. She did notice the woman, leading the meeting. She looked intelligent and rich, and Vera thought maybe she was someone to get to know, but mostly, she just felt relaxed, and she wasn't sure why. There was something about what people said that rang true with her. Still, she wasn't ready to call herself an alcoholic.

Trace told her that was fine. She might want to try another meeting the next night? To Vera that sounded extreme, but she promised him she'd show up the next week and see if she liked it.

So that's how their relationship began. Two years later they moved in together, four years later they were married, and for the next ten years, always two years apart, the had four little kids —two boys and two girls. Their names were Parker, Jennifer, Cole, and Rose.

MY FUNNY VIRGINIA

W HEN V ALLEY HEARD THAT V IRGINIA WAS CALLING HERSELF "Ginger," she almost flipped out. In the Book family, there were no nicknames except for hers, of course, and Vern's and Ronnie's. But the other girls? There would be no calling Victoria, "Tory" or "Vicky"; there would be no "Shy Vi" for Violet. Vera was too short to abbreviate and Viveca, well Viveca was gone. There would certainly be no "Ginger" for Virginia.

But Virginia was all about appearances—how things sounded, looked, and seemed. She was the only Book to have plastic surgery, long before it became popular, augmenting her perfectly propor- tioned breasts so that they loomed large and caught people's atten- tion, like bright headlights on a dark night. It was hard to look away. Later, she would fix her lips, those beautiful heart-shaped lips, so that they were wider, plumper, and actually a little hideous in their insistent smile. She had a tummy tuck, though she had no tummy, and chin lifts, wrinkle removals, and she changed the color of her hair as regularly as a chameleon walking through a crayon box. She was obsessed with the way she looked, always dieting and exercising, never content with the way she was.

"It is part of the job!" she cried as Valley chastised her for ruining one of God's perfectly good creations and turning herself into a freak show. But Ginger didn't see it like that.

"I like how I look! I think I look beautiful. Men love me. I'm traveling all over the world. You are all just jealous!"

Jealous of what? Vera thought to herself as she looked at Virginia, whose face was smeared with rivers of mascara and whose mouth was stuck open in a permanent pout like a trout that's been snagged, hook, line, and sinker.

"Besides, I have to keep up or they won't keep me on," Virginia explained.

"They" was United Airlines where Virginia had worked as a stewardess since she was eighteen years old. She had signed on as an optimistic youth, eager to "fly the friendly skies" around the world and see new people, new places, new things. It had all seemed glamorous at first, all those stops in foreign countries. And she really had been everywhere, to all the major cities in the US—New York, Washington DC, San Francisco, Los Angeles, Atlanta, Houston, St. Louis. She could go on. She had traveled abroad to London, Paris, Madrid, Stockholm, Athens, and Rome. Every trip had been an adventure, seeing the sights and shopping, eating native food, and sleeping with fellow crew members or strangers she had met on the streets. At every port of call, she sent postcards to Valley, who, at first, put them up with magnets on the refrigerator, but now kept them in a little box beside the black phone so she would have the messages handy in case anyone should call and Valley might have the opportunity to brag about Virginia's adventures. Those adventures for Virginia soon grew old. It was always the same sights, the same escargots and baklava, the same crew members with the same body odor and bad breath in the morning, smelling of cigarettes and gin.

One day, in 1983, on a flight to Houston, she was working in First Class. There she met a man who was older than she by at least forty years. He was handsome in an older guy kind of way. He had a full head of snow-white hair, piercing blue eyes, and a pencil thin smile that opened to reveal the whitest, straightest teeth. Dentures, she later learned.

"Champagne?" she said, offering him a flute, leaning over him just enough so her breasts were at lip level.

"Never touch the stuff. I'll just have orange juice, straight. On the rocks," he said with a wink as he reached out with his left hand and held her arm. She noticed that he had a thick gold band studded with diamonds on his ring finger. "Don't tell anyone. That'll be our secret."

By the end of the flight, many more secrets had been shared. He basically told her his life story.

"… married forty years to a wonderful woman who passed last year. She left me with three greedy children who have never grown up. They're waiting for me to die and leave them a fortune that they don't deserve. I made a bit in oil." He took a long sip of his juice, looking down into the cup. When he looked up, she noticed that his eyes were watery and pink, on the verge of tears. "I'm lonely. Can't really trust anyone. Everyone wants my money. But you seem like a nice girl. Can I trust you?" he asked.

As Virginia stood in the galley replenishing her supply of peanuts and club soda, she knew that this is what she had been called to do. Marry a rich man. A rich old man who would die and leave her a fortune. But she had to be careful, very careful, not to let on that she didn't love him, thought his liver spots were repulsive, and she found it hard not to turn away when he stared at her with those watery, pink-rimmed eyes. But Virginia was good, very good at pretending at being someone she was not.

So when they touched down in Houston, she helped him with his coat and bag, handed him his ten-gallon hat, and walked him to the door. As he was leaving, he kissed her on the cheek, gently pressing a business card into the palm of her hand.

"It's been a pleasure, Miss …?" he said.

"Book. Ginger Book," she said smiling back. With a tip of his hat, he was gone.

Virginia looked at the card in her hand. It was just a plain, white business card with LARRY HAWKINS written in the middle. Below was typed the word OIL, and below that, a phone number. It wasn't too much to go on, but it was a start.

THE BIG STORM

THE SKY WAS GREEN. VERN, KNOWING THIS MEANT A STORM WAS coming, gathered all the animals and his new tractor into the barn, like Noah preparing for The Flood. As the wind picked up and black clouds, like unruly eyebrows, fringed the horizon, the horses grew jittery, and the Book's one cow, Miss Maybelline, bellowed as he guided her into an empty stall. Once he had everyone safely in, he shut the doors on both ends of the barn, latched them, and pressing against the wind which was blowing fairly hard now, went into the house to join Valley, Vera, and Violet for their evening meal.

"Everything okay?" Valley asked, looking up from the cold macaroni salad she was preparing, stirring in Miracle Whip and green onions while the chicken sizzled in the deep fryer.

"It's going to be a big storm," Vern said, pulling a Schlitz out of the fridge and popping the top.

"But the cats will be okay, right?" Violet asked from where she sat at the kitchen table shucking corn.

"You and your damned cats. You'd think there's nothing but cats in this world," mumbled Vern.

"I'm sure they'll be fine," Valley soothed Violet's concerns. "They're fighters. They'd survive anything. How are you doing with those beans, Vera?" Valley asked, changing the subject.

"Great. Just great," Vera replied, still wondering if her decision to return home for the fourth of July had been a good one. She had left Trace, with whom she was now living, in their condo in Cambridge, Massachusetts. She was fairly, newly sober, and her family still triggered in her the desire to obliterate, to drown her feelings in booze, because she felt so inadequate even though she had some small success to her credit. But family could do that to you, slice you off at the knees, turn you into a needy, insecure six-year-old all over again, make you cry and ache mercilessly.

Luckily for her, there were no more questions. Just everyone doing what they did, preparing food, drinking, carrying on in silence until the food was on the table and Valley felt the need to incite polite dinner conversation.

"So, what's the latest news from our famous author?" Valley asked cheerfully, sipping on her wine.

"I'm not famous, Valley. Although, I used to think I'd be. Now I just edit celebrities' books," Vera said humbly. "It doesn't make me special. It's just what I do."

"At least you're working," Vern scowled at Violet who sat at the table with her eyes cast down picking at her food. "Go on there, then, Violet," Vern said more loudly than necessary as he popped what would now be his fifth beer. "Dive into that plate. That's what you'd like to do, isn't it?"

Violet, who had come home forty pounds lighter four months before, felt the anvil of shame and remorse press heavy on her chest. She would be the first to agree with Vern that she was fat—had blown up like a balloon since returning home—but what he didn't know was why. He didn't know about that night, one of the last night's she was a nanny for the McGinness boys, when Dorothea had taken little Jack to the emergency room with what turned out to be a burst appendix, big Jack, or Jackass as Vera had renamed him, came into her bedroom all stupid with wine and Old Spice and concern over his baby boy. That concern had quickly turned to confessions of how he felt for Violet, how he had felt for her ever since she had first started as a nanny in their home. When she refused to accept his kisses or his hands touching her body, he had picked up a big glass ashtray the size of a gardening shovel and held it over her head and told her that if she made a sound he'd kill her. He raped her. The next night when Dorothea was still in the hospital with Jack, he came in again and raped her again, this time more sober and angrier, threatening her if she ever told anyone that he would say she came on to him, the older, handsome man.

Violet was ashamed, so ashamed that she had let this happen. She convinced herself that this was in some way her fault. Isn't it always the girl's fault for being too pretty or too wholesome, so fresh that no man can resist? Think of all those Greek gods humping the nymphs they find bathing in the woods. Whose fault is that? The girls', obviously, for not hiding their beauty, for wearing provocative clothes and skin-tight bathing suits, for laughing their wide, genuine laughs, and smiling those radiant smiles. And the eyes, the violet eyes, and breasts as perfectly proportioned as rolling hills, just beckoning to be touched.

"Bullshit!" Vera yelled into the phone when Violet relayed what had happened. "He's a pig. An asshole. Leave there. Now. If you need me, I'll come and get you."

"No. I'll make my way home. But what will I tell Vern?" Violet cried.

"Tell him nothing. Tell him you're between jobs. Tell Valley you'll do whatever she needs, but don't tell Vern. He won't understand." And he didn't. He watched Violet blow up, and he grumbled about how she was costing them so much, throwing her life away. He misunderstood her need to nurture the cats and kittens as a fetish. How could he understand that she was trying to heal?

He harped at her endlessly, chiseling away any new self-esteem she might have found.

"Vern," Vera wanted to say, but something had a chokehold on her throat and nothing would come out.

"Vern," Valley whispered as Violet slowly lifted herself out of her chair, tears bouncing across her cheeks, and headed upstairs. "Apologize."

"What for?" Vern said. "She's worthless. She doesn't bring in a dime. She's 27 years old, back living at home, and she doesn't bring in a dime."

"She's troubled, and she does help around the house and the garden," Valley offered.

"Why? You don't need help around the house. You can do it yourself, if you just weren't so damned depressed and useless," he said, popping another beer.

"Vern, don't you think you've had enough?" Vera asked.

Vern snapped his gaze over to Vera. "Enough? I'll know when I've had enough and right now I've had enough of you women with your troubles and your feelings. You want to know troubles? I've got troubles. The corn is rotting. The bank is knocking at my door. I've got a dead weight daughter the size of ...."

Right then, there was a crack of lightning, a bolt so close it made Vera's teeth rattle and the hair on her arms stand on end. Vern took another gulp of his beer and then ran out the door. Vera and Valley sat rigid in their chairs until he came slamming in the screen door, yelling to them, "The barn's been hit! Call the fire department!" Then, he disappeared just as fast to set the animals free.

In the barn, the horses were frenzied, the whites of their eyes flashing as they reared up, refusing to be tethered, until Vern just opened the stall doors and let them run away. Miss Maybelline, cowering in the corner, bellowed until Vern coaxed her cautiously away from the growing flames. Kittens and cats raced like doodlebugs on the floor, pouring over the edge of the hayloft and dropping down, hysterical in the heat. Vern swooped up armfuls of cats and tossed them out into the night. He was hysterical himself watching the dry hay catch fire and the whole barn, his dream, his future, go up in flames.

By the time the fire trucks arrived, the fire was fully engaged. The roaring of the flames, the hungry heat devouring the barn like some ravenous monster, was more than Vern could bear. He sat on the porch, beer in hand, paralyzed by what he saw. The barn was encompassed in scorching white heat and around it, above it, was a shroud of thick, billowing gray smoke smeared with blue and orange and black, like some abstract paintings. In the distance, voices, firemen he assumed, yelled in and out of the rainless night.

Nolan Shepherd walked slowly up to the porch and laid his hand on Vern's shoulder, Vern who was now slumped over in his chair with his head in his hands, sobbing. When Vern looked up and saw who it was, the man who had been his wife's lover for so many years, he rose wobbling to his full height, pulled back his right arm, and punched Nolan in the face so hard that he fell down on his backside, holding his gushing nose which was clearly broken. Shaking his aching hand, Vern looked at Nolan, spat, and went inside.

CARELESS LOVE

ON A BRISK OCTOBER DAY, WITH THE SKY SO PURE AND CLEAR YOU could drink it, and slanted golden light mopping up the horizon—a day when Vern's brother Mike, who led a charmed life, would be leaf peeping in New England and traipsing around a pumpkin patch with his twin grandchildren holding his hands or picking apples so crisp that when you bit into them they spat at you and dribbled down your chin onto your hopelessly preppy alligator shirt—Vern Book sat on the porch in the rocking swing, clutching a fifth of Old Grandad and staring at the remnants of the barn that had burned down just months prior, its black silhouette sagging and misshapen, charred scales taking the place where once a cheery red had been.

There was no money for rebuilding. The insurance barely covered enough to pay off the new tractor that had been eaten by the flames. He had nowhere to keep the horses and the cow, so he sold them for a pittance, barely enough to cover groceries for a month. Violet's cats had vanished, seeking refuge elsewhere, anywhere but here in this wasteland, and for that he was glad. He had never liked the herd of them, all snarly and suspicious, running away at the least footstep on the floor, ungrateful for the roof over their heads, the food in their bellies. Come to think of it, he told himself, most things that he came into contact with ran away, like his ungrateful daughters. He was left with this big mess. The barn burned down and rotting. Valley, bedridden with diverticulitis, probably from all the smoking, bad food, and stress, at least that's what the doctors were saying. The bank, after many months of warnings, had finally sent a notice of foreclosure. It rested on his lap while he drank whiskey from the bottle, taking serious chugs, and feeling it burn down his throat and into his gut, not caring who saw or what they might think. Who were they to judge?

His life was a mess, had been a mess forever, since the war when he went to shoot photos in Germany and found himself looking into the bowels of Evil. It wasn't the heart of Evil. Evil had no heart, he thought, but Evil had bowels and claws that clutched you and dragged you into the depths of despair and there was not a God-damned thing you could do about it, he thought, chugging again until the liquid courage was gone. For a moment, he remembered Valley, how she had once seemed to be his salvation, but he had stopped worshipping her long ago, when he picked up the booze and made it his mistress, and Valley had slipped away. In his drunkenness, he thought that maybe he had had something to do with her having an affair with Nolan Shepherd, but then he came to his senses and blamed her again for all the crap that had become his life.

The day was too beautiful for Vern to sit in it. He was on a mission and he didn't want any sentimental notions of hope or redemption to get in the way of his purpose. He set down the empty bottle, leaving it by the foreclosure notice that had drifted from his lap onto the porch floor, and went inside to his study.

It was just a small room, really, at the bottom of the stairs. It once had glass French doors and lovely windows looking out on Valley's garden, but Vern had nailed plywood over the glass doors and covered the windows with dark sheets so no one could see what he was doing inside. Formerly a cozy room with a history of photographs on the walls and bookshelves full of primers on farming and encyclopedias of livestock and crops, as well as the historical novels that Vern used to enjoy, now it was a dusty, littered tangle of papers and beer cans, soiled clothes and dusty shoes.

Vern walked over to the boot box and, moving aside several pairs of muddy, thigh-high boots, pulled out another bottle of whiskey, opened it with a twist, and chugged again. It was then that he noticed a photograph that he had taken many years before, in 1960, when Viveca was being christened, a picture in which all the girls wore pink, lining up according to age, while Victoria held the bundled baby in her white christening dress as though she was a package of sausages.

"Damn it," Vern said as he tore the photograph off the wall and threw it to the floor. The glass shattered and the frame split at the seams. "Damn it!" he shouted, cursing the day they had brought the six girls into the world. None of them had turned out well, not the way he wanted them to anyway, and Viveca, his little jewel, was dead. "Damn!" he hurled a photo of himself and Valley and his brother Mike in their uniforms, laughing and smiling. What right did they have to laugh and smile? Wasn't life just a vale of tears orchestrated by a fickle god who seemed hell-bent on ruining Vern's life at every move? Drinking and smashing, he threw photos off the wall. Every time he hurled a memory, his desperation grew, he felt more and more that this whole damn thing had been a waste and the best thing would be to die.

Instead, he passed out, breaking through the glass doors and smashing his head onto the pile of broken glass. He lay limp, his right arm curled awkwardly, with blood pooling around his head, like a corpse.

"Vern?" Valley called from upstairs. "What's going on there?" When she didn't hear any response, she called out again, "Vern? Are you all right?" Again, no reply. This time, agitated and concerned, she yelled louder, propping herself up in her bed where the doctor had instructed her to stay in order to avoid blood clots moving to her heart and killing her. But when she called her husband a fourth time and got no answer, Valley pulled herself out of her bed, tied on her dark green chenille robe, slipped into the new booties Vern had bought her when the weather changed and he grew tired of massaging her icy feet, and walked gingerly to the top of the stairs.

That's when she saw him, her Vern, lying face down in a pool of blood. There was no time for blame or regret. She screamed his name and ran down the stairs. In running, she slipped on the polished soles of her new slippers and tumbled down the entire flight until she came to rest with a thump at the bottom. She didn't die right away; she was unconscious. But the clots that the doctor warned her about bubbled to her heart like gas lights at Christmas and that was enough to do her in.

Nolan Shepherd thought that this would be a fine day to visit the Books, to make amends to Vern for taking Valley away from him and to let him know that he had forgotten the incident in July when Vern hit him so hard that he not only broke Nolan's nose but his tailbone as well. He stood at the front door and wondered why it was taking them so long to answer the bell. The screen door was unlatched and the main door, too, so Nolan gave a little push and popped his head in the door. "Anybody home?" That's when he saw them: Vern lying in a pool of blood and Valley heaped at the bottom of the stairs. He quickly pulled out his revolver, which he always carried with him, thinking there might be someone lurking inside. First, he went to Valley, gently moved her long hair out of the way, and pressed his fingers against her neck, trying to get a pulse, but there was nothing. She was gone. He felt himself well up with sorrow, but he quickly shoved that down and went to Vern.

Vern had a pulse, a weak one, and when Nolan turned him over, the other man grabbed the wrist of the hand which held the gun and snatched it away from him. It all happened so quickly, Nolan later told the police, that he didn't see it coming. He thought Vern was dead, and no one was more surprised than Nolan to see him staring up with blood-shot eyes only to have him grab the gun and point it straight at Nolan.

The next seconds were a blur. Vern pulled the trigger as he held the gun to Nolan's chest but nothing happened. Then, Vern took the gun and looked into the barrel and coughed, and as he coughed he pulled the trigger and a bullet, the single bullet that Nolan kept in the chamber, flew out and took out the back of Vern's head.

The girls were told that these were accidental deaths, but Vera knew, they all knew, these were no accidents. They were the result of careless living, life without regard for life. Still, it didn't make it hurt any less.

BUZZ

THE BOOK SISTERS ARE A LOCOMOTIVE, TRAVELING FAR OFF TO THE frontier. Violet stands at the back, on the little iron porch, waving a lavender handkerchief, laughing and crying at the same time. She is waving and waving, goodbye to all that. Viveca is high above her, in a hot-air balloon, sailing toward the horizon, her pale hands gripping the basket, her dark hair flowing over the sides. She is saying something, but no one can hear. Her voice is a million miles away and caught up in the wind. Victoria is impaled on a wheel, spread eagle like Leonardo da Vinci's Vitruvian Man, and spinning, spinning in circles. Virginia walks gingerly on a tightrope carrying a yellow silk parasol with red tassels and wearing pink silk slippers as she inches along. Vera sits on a wall wondering which way she should jump, into the turbulent waters on one side, or farther through the clouds. Veronica? She stands in a dark closet, pulling the light switch off and on, off and on.

Everyone is a metaphor. Everyone is an image. Everyone is caught in the moment of being exactly who they are. The next step, the leap, will show them who they will become. Who they are meant to be. It's the leap that is the hardest, the moment before the decision is made to either cut the strings or stay imprisoned forever.

AFTERSHOCK

Valley and Vern had been laid to rest in the town cemetery, in plots on either side of their youngest daughter. The decision to separate them, have them bracket their child instead of resting side by side for eternity was not a decision that was made lightly. Valley and Vern had made no provisions for their deaths. They had left no will or instructions behind. There was no executor, and so the arrangements became a free fall, with each girl, now woman, tossing in her own two cents about how this should all be done. Eventually, the funeral director in charge suggested that every ship needs a captain, every plane a pilot, and if they got what he meant, this situation needed someone to deal with the funeral home and research the life insurance policies and take care of putting closure to their parents' lives. Despite protestations from Virginia, who asserted that she knew better than anyone how to bury the dead—hadn't she, after all, buried one husband already and done all the paperwork to take care of the next —the remaining four girls chose the next-to-oldest, Ronnie. And Ronnie felt that turning Valley and Vern into parentheses for their daughters' lives was just the metaphor that was called for. Hadn't the girls both joined and severed their relationship with their parents? The others agreed because she was Ronnie, and because Victoria who, as the eldest, should really have shouldered the responsibility, arrived at the viewing as drunk as her father used to be, only not so mean, just weepy and dumb.

Their parents' deaths in 1986 set the girls free. There was no windfall, no hidden insurance policy that gave them all a hefty lump sum to begin their new life, or pick up the old one. What there was can only be described as "whoosh!" as if 100 balloons held pinched at the nose were suddenly liberated and set flying in buzzing, random acrobatics across the sky. Suddenly free of Vern's meanness and Valley's debilitating sorrow, Violet quit her nanny jobs looking after other people's children and began looking after herself. She applied, and was admitted to, the Rhode Island School of Design, given a substantial scholarship, and initiated a career in illustration. For a number of years, she illustrated other people's books, but with encouragement from her peers, she soon forayed out on her own, writing a series of children's books with a loveable stinkbug who lived in a matchbox by the kitchen sink as her protagonist. "Wayne," as Violet called him, taught children lessons in resilience and self-love as he skirted danger daily, narrowly escaping with his life. Ugly and misunderstood, Wayne taught children to love themselves for who and what they are, not for who and what the outside world wanted them to be. Every time Violet wrote a story and drew the ink and marker sketches that went with it, every time Wayne avoided the Big Shoe that set out to squish him or the White Tissue that wanted to swallow him up and flush him down the john, she felt that she was erasing dark smudges on the pages of her past. She was rewriting the story of who she was and how she defined herself.

Violet took her brushes and sketch pad went to visit Ronnie in North Carolina where she lived with her partner, Parker Jones, and ran a veterinary clinic for everything from horses to hedgehogs. Ronnie saw immediately the change in her younger sister.

"You're lighter. Not just weight-wise," Ronnie remarked. "Your energy is lighter."

Violet grinned. "I am! I feel ... lighter!"

"Well, that's profound," Ronnie laughed and they both had a good giggle, something neither of them had enjoyed for quite a while. Necessary healing, Ronnie would call it later.

"Do you think it's bad that I'm relieved they're gone?" the lavender-eyed Violet asked as she walked with Veronica while she checked on the animals in the paddock outside.

"Do I think it's bad? No, I just think that it is. The way I figure it, I owe all those years in Iowa nothing. Valley and Vern? I owe them my life, of course, but after that, next to nothing. They were terrible parents," Ronnie said as she pulled some carrots out of her pocket and fed them to the two miniature donkeys standing in the field.

"What's wrong with these guys?" Violet asked.

"Nothing. I just keep them because I like them." Ronnie stated simply. "That's Blessing 2," she said, pointing to a beautiful bay horse, head down, munching grass in the field.

Blessing 1 had been sold for horsemeat after the barn burned down, and Ronnie would never forgive Vern for that, Ronnie told Violet. "It was just one of any number of very bad decisions he made when he drank. And he was always drunk. Ergo, he was always bad."

Violet shuddered as Ronnie spoke. She hated to hear that her parents were bad. She had seen bad parents, worked for them, next to them. They abused their children psychologically and sometimes physically. But Valley and Vern? What did they do? Nothing. That was just it, they turned their attention to other things—booze, politics, cigarettes, worries about money—and they left their six daughters to grow up on their own. Look how they had all grown.

After many years of rotating relationships, Victoria, the eldest of the Book sisters, had finally settled on being single. The afternoon that her divorce from husband number two was complete, she walked herself into the nearest bar, sat down on a stool at the counter, and ordered herself a double Tanqueray on the rocks with a twist of lime. She lamented ever getting into that relationship, but she had been taken in by his smooth talk and attractive façade. For years they lived in suburban Connecticut. She stayed home trying on various roles that never suited her— gardening, bridge, dinner clubs—while he dealt in art. It wasn't until she came home one afternoon and found the house surrounded by cop cars, lights flashing, sirens mute. The next thing she knew, her ex (she couldn't even say his name) was being escorted out of the house in handcuffs. It was only later that she found out that he was trafficking in stolen goods. Of course, she drank. Victoria thought. Who wouldn't?

The bar was almost empty, dark and so quiet that you could hear the hum of the Budweiser clock over the glasses behind the bar. The bartender, not wanting to intrude in Victoria's space, stood quietly still, wiping glasses clean with a soft, white cloth.

The door to the bar opened and let in a box of yellow light and the whine of cars passing by on the street outside. In walked a tall man in tight black pants with a red silk tunic top trimmed in gold. He sat down at the bar one seat away from Victoria and ordered several shots, which he downed like peanuts, and rapped on the counter for another round.

"So, what do you do?" he asked Victoria.

"I beg your pardon?" she replied.

"What are you, the Queen? I asked you what you do and I asked because I have a purpose," he said, finishing his shots and then rapping on the bar again. Victoria ignored him, sipping her drink and then tapping on the counter with two fingers for another drink. "I need a woman," he said.

"Just what do you think I am?" Victoria said indignantly.

"Not that kind of a woman," the man laughed. "I need a woman for my act."

Victoria sipped her drink, her interest piqued. "And what exactly is your act?" she asked.

"I throw knives. For the circus."

"Really?" Victoria said and faced him as she felt a shiver run down her spine and into her toes. "That's so exciting!" And, indeed she was excited and mildly turned on by the idea that this man with the swarthy skin and square jaw and eyes that were blacker than night, threw knives at someone, potentially lethally, for a living. She had thrown plenty of knives, plates, and glasses in her time, always in a fit of rage and usually under the influence, but she'd never made money doing it. Or, come to think of it, she'd never been on the receiving end. "So, you want me to let you throw knives at me?" she asked.

"Yeah. You'd wear a little red corset with black lace and garters, and fishnet stockings and high heels. I can see from looking at you that it would all look very good on you, if I do say so myself."

Victoria laughed, ordered a third drink which she didn't bother sipping, she just downed in one swallow. She wasn't immune to flattery, and the idea of running away to join the circus was just wild and improbable enough to catch her fancy. But one question begged to be asked. "What happened to your last lovely assistant?"

The man knocked back three more shots, looked Victoria straight in the eye, and said "I slipped."

"And is she? Did she?" Victoria managed to ask once her heart stopped pounding so boldly it shook her blouse.

The man nodded and ran his finger across his throat.

Victoria motioned for another drink. The very fact that she was even considering this proposition should have told her that it was time to run. She had received no settlement from her recent ex, but her son, Artie had told her she had a place to stay until she was settled. Her life could be on a good track. She could go back to her music, playing and teaching. It could all be normal, whatever that was, and serene. But Victoria was not about being serene. Victoria thrived on chaos, she welcomed distractions as a shark welcomes a school of fish, feeding off it, devouring it. At this very moment, she felt no obligations to her son or to her sisters or to her future.

She was, if anything, totally selfish, and so she agreed to go with the man to the circus to become his assistant. At thirty-eight years old, without parents, without a spouse, without a job, without a plan, this seemed to be the most sensible course of action Victoria could take.

Back in North Carolina, Ronnie continued her rounds with Violet in tow.

"She really joined the circus?" Violet asked, astonished.

"That's what I heard," Ronnie replied.

"Who told you? Virginia?"

"Of course. The source of all gossip."

"She has made it her job to keep up on all of us through the years. Of course, she never contacts me," Violet whined.

"Get over it," Veronica advised. "It's her loss."

No one really understood the fifth daughter, Virginia, and who could? She kept herself so tightly wrapped in folds of personality, like a Russian doll that you revealed one by one, each doll getting smaller and more compact as you went along until you were left with the tiniest, tightest little creation. That was Virginia. On the surface, she was all bluster and compatibility. She was everyone's friend, knew everyone's business. She was conscientious about sending birthday cards and other greetings; for a while there had been Christmas gifts too. Vera believed this was Virginia's way of controlling what everyone thought of her, because she'd made some pretty suspect choices. Like her first marriage.

At twenty-one, she had a set of artificial boobs that cost her more than she made in a month, but which she was sure sent the message she wanted to send to any man who met her. So why was she surprised when Vincent Delgado turned out to be just as false as she? By day, he was a successful Boston lawyer; at night, when he drank, he turned into Mr. Hyde, physically abusing her with anything he could find in the house to throw at her. Emotionally abusing her as he shouted profanities and called her names. This was a woman that those who thought they knew Virginia knew nothing about.

This was Virginia the martyr who suffered through this abuse just as Valley had suffered Vern's abuse. Neither knew any better. And neither knew how to fight back.

When Vincent attacked her with a broken bottle, tearing the right side of her face and almost blinding her with the jagged glass, she told the doctor in the emergency room that she had been attacked by a German Shepherd. Of course, he didn't believe her, but he sent her to a plastic surgeon who patched up her face anyway. Without a word. Virginia could neither have confronted Vincent nor left him, no matter what the surgeon said. Her husband was a boozing man, and very rich, and it wasn't even that she felt powerless or afraid of him. She felt numb. She felt this very old familiarity with a situation over which she had no control, and she felt that she had no options. A young woman with no connections to family on a pittance of a salary? Where was she to go except into the arms of a wealthy man? She felt that she had no other choice.

She found him dead from an overdose when she came home from work one weekend. She couldn't say that she was sorry. She wasn't. Vincent was mean, Vern mean. It was good that he was gone. But still, she had wanted a man in her life to take care of her and he was the first to volunteer. Mercifully, he left her quite a bit of money, enough for a new face, a new wardrobe, and a new life. She kept her job. She had always liked her job.

Virginia had arrived at Viveca's funeral wrapped in a voluminous fox stole, showing off that she was rich and successful, but hiding the scars on her body, never sharing her secrets.

"You seem to be doing pretty well for yourself," Vera commented to Virginia as they powdered their noses in the extremely floral women's room at the funeral home.

"I'm doing great!" Virginia replied too enthusiastically, as she wiped off the mascara streaks that ran down her cheeks and reapplied the thick liner.

"Miss Maybelline!" the sisters laughed in unison, and then Virginia dissolved into tears again. Vera just let her cry, imagining that she was overwhelmed with grief over the loss of their youngest sister, Virginia's "twin."

"They say it would have been quick," Vera offered.

"What?" Virginia said as she blew her nose in a Kleenex.

"The accident. They say if she hadn't done what she did, that mother and those two little girls would have been killed." This information made Virginia howl with grief and bawl even harder.

"She was so good!" Virginia cried. "So good. I'm not so good. I'm bad."

"What do you mean?" Vera asked, but Virginia wouldn't tell her.

"I'm fine. I'm good. Just needed a cry. Let's go out there, shall we, and entertain the troops. Viveca wouldn't want us all to be long-faced and mourning. She's where she always wanted to be. With Jesus. We should be happy for her."

Vera looked at her sister incredulously, not believing a word of the shit she was spouting.

HAPPY TRAILS

As Ronnie, the second Book daughter, and Parker, her partner, worked together to patch up a particularly mangled sweet old pit bull that had been hit and run over by a speeding truck full of teenagers, whooping it up, throwing empty glass bottles onto the road, and waving a giant Confederate flag, Ronnie felt her enthusiasm failing. She had seen so many sweet animals, victims of human carelessness and abuse, die on her table. She feared that "Lacey," as her owner had called her, might be the next to go.

"Penny for your thoughts?" her partner asked her as Ronnie stitched around the puddles of blood that Parker mopped up as fast as she could. Nothing could help this poor animal now.

"Nothing," she replied and carried on, determined to give Lacey her best effort.

"Nothing as in really nothing," or "nothing I want to share," Parker prodded.

"I'm just tired, Parks, tired of everything dying. Can't we do something fun once in a while?" Ronnie asked uncharacteristically.

And that's how they got into hiking the Appalachian Trail. At first, it was just day trips to Bald Mountain and Laurel Gorge. In the spring, the trail was bordered by heaping azaleas, orange, pink, yellow, and white. The rhododendrons had scarlet blossoms as big as balloons. The hills and mountains were still close-cropped with short grass, not yet covered with the wildflowers that would come in summer and the tall grasses that sang with insects and swayed in the wind.

As they hiked along the trails, they met others who, like them, were seeking refuge from the heaviness of life, a heaviness that was lifted once they placed one foot after the other on the dusty trail, finding a rhythm and walking under the clear blue sky. Sometimes there were clouds. Fat, muscular clouds that took a thousand shapes: a belly dancer, a sleeping bear, a bowler, a gaggle of ducklings, a dolphin leaping into the air. Ronnie and Parker played games with what they saw, making up stories and giggling like the lovers they were, stealing kisses under the golden sun.

One day in October they were hiking the trails. The air was crisp and smelled of autumn, moist leaves and dying grasses and sweet apples rotting in the sun. But there were no apple trees, only memories of the Fall in their youth when everything smelled like candy corn. The houses were all decorated with pumpkins, gourds, and bales of straw, and the heady smell of chrysanthemums filled the air. October meant Halloween and Halloween meant fun, dressing up to fulfill fantasies of being a pirate or a gypsy or Robin Hood in electric green tights.

"This is perfect," Parker cooed as they made their way along the trail. "A perfect fall day."

Ronnie smiled but said nothing as she walked along, swinging her walking stick out in front of her with purpose, lost in her own lazy gait.

"Penny?" Parker chirped.

"Nothing. Just looking," Ronnie replied.

"It is so beautiful," Parker agreed as she nearly slammed into Ronnie who had stopped dead in her tracks, her hand held up like an Indian scout.

"What is it?" Parker asked, concerned.

"Do you hear that?" Ronnie asked quietly. Parker listened but heard nothing.

"I don't hear it," she said.

"Sure, you do. Listen."

Parker listened more intently, even stopping her own breathing so she would be perfectly still. It was quiet. So quiet. The only sound was the sweep of the wind in the grass which made a very low whistling song. Elsewise, the sky was empty. No birds. No voices. No feet scrunching on dirt. Just quiet. "I don't hear anything," she confessed.

"Exactly. Nothing. The perfect place for this," Ronnie said, taking Parker by the hand and leading her through the tall grass that fringed the trail to the meadow filled with little flying things. Very gradually and deliberately, Ronnie took off her jacket and laid it on the ground. Then, she took off her long-sleeved T-shirt and unbuckled her shorts and stood there in front of Parker in her underwear.

"Your turn," she said simply and Parker obliged eagerly. Before you knew it, they were lying naked in the sun, the blue sky overhead and the tall grass shielding them as they kissed and touched one another fondly, knowing just how to bring pleasure to one another.

"Now this is perfect," Ronnie said, taking Parker's face into her hands and kissing the woman she loved deeply, with passion.

Their moment was interrupted when they heard some rustling in the grasses and then a steady hiss. Instinctively, Parker started to leap up, grabbing her shirt, and clutching it to her breasts, but Ronnie pulled her down, putting a finger over her lips.

"What if it's a snake?" Parker whispered.

"That's no snake," Ronnie hissed back. "Get dressed."

Before they could fasten their bras and buckle their belts, the tall grasses parted and standing before them was a man, probably 6'8", muscular and darkly tanned, wearing camouflage pants and a black T-shirt. The bulging muscles in his arms were covered with tattoos and he had one word etched across his forehead: EVIL.

Ronnie breathed a long, slow breath, certain that this was no early trick-or-treater. Parker reached out and grabbed Ronnie's hand. They had heard about situations like this, a couple of women, encountering such a man. Usually, it didn't end well. Ronnie assessed the situation—her little walking stick and her 5'6", 135-pound frame against this giant of a man who sported a hunting knife on one hip and God knew what else. For a moment, she was afraid.

"Afternoon," she spoke up with as much bravado as she could muster. "Beautiful day."

The man looked at her, at them, with lascivious eyes, actually more bloodthirsty than lascivious. "You ladies enjoying yourselves?" He grinned.

"Great day for a hike," Ronnie replied.

"Yeah. Right," the man chuckled, fingering his knife. "You lesbos?" he asked.

"As a matter of fact, we are," Ronnie responded honestly, figuring he must have seen them rolling around together and what else was he to think. No point in lying.

"You know what we do to lesbos around her, don't you?"

Parker let go with a little gasp, her hand flying to cover her mouth.

"I'd like to think you just let us be on our way," Ronnie replied.

"Some folks slit their throats, some folks shoot 'em between the eyes. Some folks rape 'em, gag 'em, and leave 'em there to die."

A murder of crows sailed across the sky, cawing and calling, their cries echoing in the otherwise silent air. Sweat beaded on Ronnie's brow and she wiped it off carelessly, though inside she certainly wondered where this was all going. Was this how she and Parker were going to die? Fileted on a mountaintop, left to die in the golden autumn sun?

Suddenly, a clatter of voices burst up the trail and a party of a dozen hikers, all happy and chatting, emerged around the bend. Ronnie reached down for Parker, grabbing her and what little clothing they could, and made a break toward the crowd yelling, "Hey wait! Wait for us!"

As Ronnie ran, she dropped her stick, turned to reach down and get it. When she looked up at the monster man, he was singing in a low, penetrating voice:

"Happy Trails to you, until we meet again
Happy Trails to you, keep smiling until then.
Happy Trails to you 'til we meet again."

Never one to give up the last word, Ronnie raised not one, but two, middle fingers at him and then disappeared into the crowd.

The incident sent a chill through the women's bodies, but it did not deter them from continuing their hikes, armed with whistles and pepper spray from then on. May of the next year, 1988, they heard that two lesbians had been shot while hiking, Rebecca Wright and Claudia Bronner, because some whack job had come across them hugging on the trail. Ronnie and Parker each returned to that moment the previous fall. "He could have killed us," Parker whispered as Ronnie held her close. "We could be dead."

Ronnie soothed her and then, the very next day, announced her plan to hike the entire Appalachian Trail. Not by themselves, though. This was going to be an Event, a "Dyke Hike" as Ronnie called it. With the help of her sisters throughout the country, she intended to flood the Appalachian Trail from Georgia to Maine with lesbians, gays, bisexuals, and transgenders, flushing out the bigots and assholes who smeared black paint on their faces and terrorized innocent people who had every right to be walking in the woods, for God's sake, to be living on this planet as they did.

Parker listened to her agitated lover. She was drawn in by Ronnie's enthusiasm and conviction. She knew that when Ronnie had an idea, she would stick to it and there was no doubt that it would be a success. But gathering a hundred thousand LGBTs on the Appalachian Trail (AT)? How was she going to get them there, keep them there without destroying the very trail they were trying to safeguard?

"Who said a hundred thousand?" Ronnie asked Parker.

"You said 'flood the trails.' I saw a hundred thousand," Parker replied.

"I was thinking 25,000, straight and gay combined."

"OK," Parker sighed. "That sounds more reasonable. So figure about 10,000. How are you going to get them there? Travel in mass?"

Ronnie shook her head. "It's not going to be 10,000 at once. Not everyone will hike from Georgia to Maine. We will be the core group, us and about 20 others, and we'll add people on and drop them off as we go along."

"That sounds reasonable," Parker repeated. "But how are you going to advertise this event?"

"Did you ever see *White Christmas* with Bing Crosby and Danny Kaye?" Ronnie asked.

"Of course! It was my mother's favorite!"

"Well I'm going to pull a Bing Crosby. I'm going to look up my old friends, Steph and Sam, who are in the TV business and I'm going to ask for their help," Ronnie grinned. "They know Johnny Carson and I'm hoping they'll get us on."

"Us?"

"I am the brains but you're the beauty. Together we can sell this thing." Parker was silent for a few minutes, then she looked up at Ronnie with her green-gold eyes flashing, her long tawny hair backlit by the sun, and she said, "I'm the brains too."

To which Ronnie just replied, "Of course you are." On a foggy morning in late March 1989, Ronnie, Parker, Steph, Sam, and an assortment of 25 gay and lesbian men and women set off from Springer, Georgia, to hike the whole AT. Their party included two physicians, four college professors, a pilot, several teachers, two ball-room dancers, a psychic, and a cameraman and his crew. Peter Jeffries was there to document the hike, to catch on film the beauty and the camaraderie, but also to record any unpleasant incidents they might encounter along the way. Though no protesters or bigots had seen them off on their journey, Ronnie was sure that word would spread and they would be met with resistance as they went. And they were prepared. Every member of the core party had received instruction and was carrying cans of pepper spray and walking sticks. Ronnie had wanted them all to pack pistols, but it was too complicated with all the different conceal and carry rules in the fourteen states.

Hiking through Georgia in late March, they saw the advent of spring. The air and light were cool and clear, the sun almost citric with its lemony tone. Along the trail, the first birds whistled their rocking songs and the trillium curled up scarlet and green from the ground. May apples congested the forest floor, their leaves like little star shaped umbrellas. Everything smelled earthy and sweet, the perfume of Life, a smell that Ronnie adored. She loved the mockingbirds in the trees and the slices of sunlight illuminating the path under the canopy of branches. She loved the rhythm of walking and the sound of her own breathing that washed inside her like the tide. Walking quietly, without talking, allowed her to think, and as they made their way up the trail, from Georgia into South Carolina and farther into North Carolina, she found she was holding back from the big crowd that chatted endlessly and sang silly hiking songs, and she thought.

She thought about the town they had stopped in overnight to pick up supplies and rest for a while and how they were met with people holding signs, chanting "No Queers Here!" How they had been bombarded with rotten food and had to retreat to the trail and hope that the next stop was friendlier. When she was growing up, she had asked Vern about his time in the war. They were out mucking stalls one day and slinging soiled straw into a wheelbarrow.

"Not much to talk about. People were mean," Vern had replied.

"Mean like what?" Ronnie, who had been learning about the Holocaust in her history class, asked.

"Evil mean. Killing innocent people. Women and children. All because they were Jews." Then, Ronnie asked the unthinkable question.

"What did you do about it, Vern?"

Vern put his pitchfork down and leaned on it heavily, looking Ronnie straight in the eyes.

"What did I do about it? What could I do about it? I took pictures, tried to show the world. When it was all over I bought this farm, married your mother, and swore that I would keep you safe from all that. How am I doing?" he smiled weakly.

Ronnie remembered that weak smile as she walked along the trail. How was he doing? He was a lousy farmer, a lousy husband, a lousy father who drank himself drunk every night and wasted his life away. But suddenly, walking along this trail with this band of misfits who society didn't seem to want, she understood. He just got tired and he lost hope. Well, she was tired. Tired of being met at towns by angry mobs, people who must have thought that if you got too near a lesbian you'd become one too. She was tired and hungry and she could have used a good sleep, but she knew she needed to keep going. To bring the message to the world that the LBGT community was not one of lepers or social deviants. It was filled with smart, caring, capable individuals who simply lived in another sexual reality than most of the world.

Somewhere in Virginia they were joined by an older man, in his late 60s probably, who was on sabbatical from a teaching post at a divinity school in New England. He wasn't with them long, but while he was with them he spoke to them about the rise of the Religious Right. He warned, a voice crying in the wilderness, that this movement would take over our political system if they were not stopped and would set us back hundreds of years with their small-minded prejudice against anything that was not white and male. They called themselves Christians, and yet they were about as far from loving their neighbors as a person could be. They feasted on divisiveness and conflict. They devoured hate.

The Marshall, as several in the crowd had dubbed him, preached while some listened intently and asked what they could do. But most, enjoying the bucolic landscape with rolling pastures dotted with Tootsie Roll-shaped bales of hay, simply swatted his dire predictions away, burying their heads in the sands of complacency, certain that this march would make the statement that the world would heed and ignoring the fact that outside their cozy hiking party, the natives were restless, filling their pots with oil and banging the dinner drum.

The showdown came not in the South where Ronnie had expected it, but in New Jersey, at High Point State Park. It was late August by the time the group reached there, and the light slung low and golden, but the air was still blazing as it had been most of the summer with temperatures projected to reach high into the 90s by mid-day. Or so a mounted park ranger told them.

The dedicated band, now comprising about two dozen including a young man named Colin who was suffering from AIDS and was making a last stand before he perished, made their way slowly along the trail. Little was said. There were just the sounds of crunching stones under feet and walking sticks slapping rocks and pushing large pebbles out of the way. The trees overhead formed a canopy that sheltered them from the sun, though shafts of light pierced through the branches and dappled the path. Some leaves were already turning. Flashes of yellow and orange popped through the green. In the meadows the tall milkweed rose, purple with many blossoms jutting from their stalks. Soon the pods would form, like lime-colored canoes, and then the silky parachutes of silvery white strands would fly off into the sky, held by a single dark button. The goldenrod, arched stems speckled with burnished yellow flowers, swayed in the breeze, and the leaves of the sumac were blushing scarlet already, a leafy cone around the velvety red fruit. Ronnie wondered if they would meet their deadline of October 1st to reach Mount Katahdin in Maine. They had had some delays along the way—twisted ankles, diarrhea, and the mobs. Always the mobs. But there hadn't been any trouble for a while, she thought. Maybe now that they were farther north, the troubles would go away.

No sooner had she thought this, then trouble found them again. It was EVIL, or could have been, except this time there were half-a-dozen men just like him, dressed in black T-shirts and camouflage pants, curved hunting knives in their pockets and. black paint smeared along their cheeks. Ronnie held up her hand and the hikers stopped. The two groups looked at each other for several minutes without a word. It could have been a pastoral scene, the leaves falling softly from the trees, the one bird calling lightly through the air, and the crickets chirping like sleigh bells. But it was not. The air was thick with tension as the hikers took out their pepper spray and the intruders fingered their knives.

"We don't want any trouble," Ronnie said.

"We do," the leader replied. And with that, the men in black raced toward the hikers, whooping and slashing. It wasn't clear whether they were intending to frighten or to harm, but the hikers fought back valiantly, spraying mace and swinging sticks, to little avail. Several ran to get help. By the time the park rangers had arrived and rustled up the bad guys, Colin was dead and many more were injured, including Parker who had tried to fend the bad guys off of Ronnie, but ended up with a concussion, contusions, and abrasions all over her body, a dictionary of abuse. Ronnie escaped with a strained hamstring, two black eyes, and a broken rib, but she was even more determined to finish the trail.

"Not now," Parker, who was lying in a hospital bed, reached out for Ronnie's hand. "Please, not now," she implored as she lay there, wrapped like a mummy and swollen like a plum.

"If not now, when?" Ronnie asked. "We can't let them win. What about Colin? We can't let them get away with that."

"It's out of our hands, Ronnie. The Coroner said he died of a heart attack, natural causes. He was very sick."

"He wouldn't have had a heart attack if those assholes hadn't ambushed us," Ronnie fumed.

"You're probably right," Parker conceded, "but there's nothing we can do. Still, they didn't win. They'll never win, not as long as we have each other," Parker said, squeezing Ronnie's hand.

"They win if we don't fight."

"They win if we do."

And that's how they left it, with Ronnie mad but resigned, and Parker satisfied that Ronnie wasn't marching to her death. Some things are just important to lose to a cause, Parker thought, and love is one of them.

After a long period of quiet accompanied only by the hum of the florescent lights and the occasional ping of the machine that Parker was attached to, Ronnie broke the silence. This thing wasn't over yet. It couldn't be, not for her. If she caved now, giving up and hiding away ostrich-like with the woman she loved, she would be just like her father, and she didn't want that. Drunk and depressed, he'd spent his life hiding from the truth, that he had deserted and sought the easier, softer way. Truly, he would have been better off living a life chasing images of evil and despair and posting them for the world to see. As it was, his inner demons chased him to death's door, which was not where Ronnie saw herself heading. She knew that Parker would object and might leave her altogether, but she had to stick to her course. Some things were too important to lose, and Being True to Yourself was one of them.

"I'm not giving up," she said simply.

"I never thought you would," Parker replied.

"I'm going to disband the crew, send them all home, but then I'm finishing the hike." Parker closed her eyes and breathed softly through parted lips. "I don't expect you to come with me."

"Of course, I'm coming with you. If we are going down, we are going down together," she smiled.

"No one is going down. We'll just be two women hiking the trail. No press. No fanfare. Just us." Ronnie took Parker's hand and squeezed it hard. "I have to do this, Parks."

"I know you do."

After Colin's funeral, the women got back on the trail, with little time to spare. Winter would be coming soon, and by the time they reached Maine there might be snow. The nights were already cold, but Parker wouldn't let them zip their sleeping bags together lest someone come across them and see them cuddling. Ronnie didn't see the point, but she went along with Parker's wishes anyway, and as they entered towns or came across other hikers, they maintained a respectful distance so as not to attract attention, though attention is what Ronnie truly desired. Or did she? As she hiked along the trail under golden skies or in the cold November rain, she thought. What did she really want from life? Did she really want to fight battles and save lives? She felt as though she had seen enough death to last her a lifetime. What she really wanted to do was heal, heal troubled souls. She thought back to her childhood when she had helped birth Blessing, her first foal, and how she and Blessing had grown together until she left. Then, Vern had sold Blessing for what, she knew not, though she guessed that Blessing, being old, had gone for glue or dog food. It broke her heart to think of that as Blessing's end, her horse who had given her so much comfort and love, galloping through the fields bareback, the wind in her hair or just nuzzling and being nuzzled by those soft, floppy lips. Her best times, the best times of her life had been with horses, and it was horses, horses as healers and healing horses that made her heart beat just a little bit faster, telling her that she was onto something that would be good for her soul,

After a brief stop in Monson, Maine, to eat, sleep, shower and prepare for the last rugged one hundred miles of the trip, Ronnie and Parker got back on the trail again. It was their goal to reach

Mount Katahdin in two weeks, an event both women were looking forward to with anticipation. Ronnie had a special surprise planned for the summit, a secret which she kept as she proposed to Parker, not that they marry but rather that they expand their business. With the cash that she and Parker had saved from the veterinary clinic, Ronnie could afford to buy some land in North Carolina and open a haven for old, injured, and abused horses. She had this idea that if she opened the barns and pastures to people who loved horses and just wanted to be around the animals, not to ride them but to groom them and love them, people who were willing to do a little work with the maintenance of the stalls and grounds, they could stay afloat on the contributions made by the "guests" and help out the animals in the long run.

While it seemed like a strange idea to Parker at first—who would want to pay to come do work? — she agreed to support Ronnie and maintain the vet clinic while Ronnie ran the farm. How could she refuse? She loved this woman with all her heart, loved her tenacity, her vision, her soul. She owed Ronnie at least her life as the other woman had saved her from sure death and encouraged her on the trail when she had been ready to give up.

"You can't give up now," Ronnie said, pulling Parker up by both arms from where she had sat down exhausted on a slab of rock.

"But I'm so tired and this is so hard," Parker whined.

"Stop complaining and get up. This isn't hard. This is life. You just have to keep going one step at a time," Ronnie coached, as much for herself as her partner. "Just pretend you're a mailman delivering a letter to the summit. Neither rain, nor snow, nor sleet, nor hail."

The very notion struck Parker as very funny and she hoisted herself up, ready to deliver the imaginary letter. "Can't keep the mailman from delivering the mail," she laughed, finishing Ronnie's thought. And on they walked over the last grueling miles of mountain and rocks until they reached their destination—the rectangular wood placard with the word Katahdin carved into it. At that point

Ronnie pulled out a flag and collapsible pole from her backpack and planted it firmly at the top of the mountain. The wind whipped the rainbow flag and set it flapping in the sky. Ronnie looked at Parker, who took her hands and said quietly, "We did it." Ronnie wrapped Parker in her arms and hugged her tightly.

"We did," she said. "Now how the hell do we get home?"

A BETTER LIFE

THE LAVENDER-EYED VIOLET, NOW 30 YEARS OLD, HAD MADE HER way through a minor blizzard, down Commonwealth Avenue, past all the Christmas wreaths and bells and lights that were perpendicular in the wind, to her psychiatrist's office. She was that desperate, and that dedicated, for help. Though her life had taken a turn for the better and she was enjoying some success with her illustrated books, she couldn't shake the heaviness that accompanied her everywhere, and not the heaviness of the extra fifty pounds she carried on her frame. This heaviness was more than simple depression, it was existential despair. She felt to her core that there was no hope for her, no bright future waiting around the corner. When she saw people carrying armloads of brightly wrapped Christmas presents, laughter in their voices and merriment in their eyes, she blanched, wondering what it must feel like to be so carefree. Merry Christmas meant nothing to her. She knew she would eat too much, sit in the corner at Vera's house and nurse her spiked eggnog and gaze, baffled, at the cozy scene. Where had she gone wrong?

When she entered the psychiatrist's office, all gray and blue with brown accents, she wanted to run. The song from "Rudolph, the Red-Nosed Reindeer" about the "Land of the Misfit Toys" was playing over the intercom. That's what she was, a misfit. Not a misfit like the gorgeous Marilyn Monroe, but a mousy misfit who floated from home to home minding other people's children with no hope ever of having her own.

Cut the crap, she told herself. Get off the pity pot. Look at the bright side. Was there a bright side? Maybe. There was a man sitting in the waiting room with her, sketching. She didn't want to intrude but she did glance down as she passed by his chair. The sketches were of flying horses and clouds and angels, and they were good. Here they were in the waiting room, the only two, and they were both artists escaping into their art. What were the chances? He muttered something loudly under his breath.

"Pardon? Were you talking to me?" Violet asked defensively.

"Oh, no, sorry. I was just saying that this song is like us. In here. Wounded. Broken," he said.

Violet wasn't sure if she approved of being called broken by a man she didn't even know. She sat as tall and still as she could in her layers of clothing until she felt the sweat bead on her brow. Her head felt light, as if she might swoon.

"I'd take all that stuff off if I were you, before you faint," came the voice from the artist with the book.

How could he have known? Violet wondered. He didn't even look up. Gingerly, she removed her hat, her gloves, and slowly uncoiled the scarf, so relieved when she felt the cooler air on her neck. Again, she could breathe. Finally, she unbuttoned her overcoat and opened it wide.

"Feel better?" he asked.

"Much, thanks," she replied.

"Ben?" the doctor said as he opened the door to the inner sanctum. "You ready?

Ben closed his sketchbook and placed it in his satchel, stood up, and walked to the door. As he moved across the room, Violet noticed that he was tall, very tall, and apparently well built. The muscles of his lean thighs pressed against his jeans and his stomach was as flat as hers was round. His skin was very pale, luminous almost, and his eyes were as green as a cat's. He had beautiful hands.

Violet wished that she were thin and attractive, that she could attract someone like him, a man who was so handsome and intuitive. But what did she really know about him? He was in a psychiatrist's office too! Maybe he had raped someone and needed to confess, only he wasn't Catholic so he sought psychiatric relief instead. Stop! Violet told herself, picking up a woman's magazine. Stop judging, stop looking at the world through that filter of violence and negativity. Give the man a chance. So, she dove into an article on Christmas cookies which caught her attention because Vera's kids would be home for Christmas vacation and that might be her gift to them.

Before she had time to assimilate the recipe for toffee bars into her brain, the door opened and Ben stepped out. He turned to the doctor, shook his hand, and said, "Merry Christmas."

"Merry Christmas to you, Ben. See you in six months. Violet? Violet Book?" the doctor called.

Violet, who had taken off her coat by now, scooped up her winter wear, and glided past Ben, looking at him quickly with her amazing violet eyes. Their gaze caught for a second and then she walked on into the cozy office outfitted with a leather couch and chairs, old books, and paintings, all presumably by the same artist, of oceans and boats at rest and boats at sea. Violet vaguely remembered something from high school English, an Edgar Lee Masters poem from *Spoon River Anthology*. Something about a boat at rest in a harbor and how we must catch the winds of destiny wherever they lead us.

"To put meaning in one's life may end in madness/but life without meaning is like a boat longing for the sea and yet afraid," she murmured.

"I beg your pardon?" the doctor, a slight man with the twinkle of an elf, said.

"Oh, sorry. Was I saying that aloud? It's your paintings. They reminded me of something."

"Tell me about it," he encouraged her. She began. She told him of the health problems she had suffered for so many years. She told him about the feelings of self-doubt and jealousy, depression and despair. She told him about her frustration with her weight and her eating, about her sisters, and her feeling that she never got the attention that she deserved. The death of her parents. The rapes. She told him that she was afraid that she would never find true love. When she was done, he looked at her with compassion and said, "You are carrying a heavy load, none of which is your fault. You truly have been a victim of circumstance."

How glad she was to hear those words, glad that he had not said to her, "You are so hard on yourself. You just need to lighten up. Don't take yourself so seriously," as she had heard so many times before. Here was a doctor who agreed with her. She wasn't at fault. She was a victim. So now, what?

"So now what do I do? Is there some magic pill I can take?" she asked.

"No medicine that I can prescribe will fix you. I think you'd do well to find a good therapist." He scribbled down several names on a pad and handed it to her. "Interview them all. Choose the one you like best. Aside from that, my only advice is to play. Do something fun every day. That shouldn't be too hard with it being the holidays and all. Indulge now, diet later. Laugh. Spread good cheer. Make clove oranges with your nieces and build snow couples on the lawn. Don't take it all so seriously," he said as he ushered her out of the office.

Violet was dumbfounded and just a little annoyed. Here was a doctor in whom she had confided the deepest secrets of her life and he had told her not to take herself too seriously, to make snowmen! Well, that certainly wasn't worth the $85 she had just spent.

As she stepped back into the waiting room, she saw that Ben was still there. He turned and looked at her, smiling. She returned the look, glancing at him with wonder and a little concern. Was this guy a freak? Was everyone in this office off their rockers? He walked over to her, holding out his hand.

"I'm Ben," he said, "Ben Bigger." Violet thought, there are so many things that I could say right now, but she didn't. "In case you are wondering, I'm here because I am bipolar, but I've been on my meds for years and I'm stable, so no fears." He sighed. "I waited for you because," he stammered slightly, "I'd like to take you to lunch. Would you like to go to lunch with me?"

In fact, Violet was starving so the notion of eating with a handsome man while taking to heart the doctor's suggestion that she do something fun every day, all worked together quite well. She found herself smiling and nodding, "Yes." As she wrapped herself back up in her coat and scarves, this time with his help, he asked her, "Do you like fondue?"

Violet grinned, stating "It's my favorite." And off she went with her new friend.

Some months later, in the spring, Vera received a postcard from Las Vegas. It showed a picture of a cheesy wedding chapel with inserts of wedding couples smooching and tossing bouquets. On the reverse side was a message which read "We eloped!!!!!" in purple ink, and signed Violet and Ben Bigger. At first Vera had no idea who it was, but then she understood. Violet had finally found her man. The bigger the better, she smirked, not missing the irony in her sister's new last name. *Don't be catty*, Vera, she told herself and planned to call Virginia who would surely know all the details of the event and where she should send a gift. But not today. She wouldn't call today. She couldn't call today. They may have all been set free by Valley and Vern's deaths, but the intricacies of communication were still a tangled web among the six sisters, and phone calls were never easy. So much misunderstanding clogged the wires. She'd save it for another day.

MIND GAMES

Vera woke restless in the night. There was no reason for it. Valley and Vern were long gone, and with them the horrors of her youth. She had miraculously survived the chaos and come out of it sober, with a husband, four kids, and a career. She lay in bed, trying to be very still and to focus on all that she had to be grateful for—the family, the house, the yard, the Japanese maples just now turning crimson, the vacations at the beach and in Vermont, her health— but always her mind wanted to race forward, dipping and swerving like a kite in a very strong wind. It galloped toward the finish line, though what was there, she did not know. She felt as if she was in a runaway stagecoach, her heart pounding, her muscles tensing, the horses chasing down disaster. She rose out of her crumpled bedding and went to the kitchen to make herself a cup of herb tea. Then, she sat in front of the quiet hearth, with Scholar, their 7-year-old Golden Retriever, lying at her feet.

Vera felt as if the wind was changing. For so many months, she had been depressed, after Parker was born, not long after her parents' deaths. She had experienced little love for the baby, even a sense of disgust and irritability that Parker had come in to her life and presented yet another distraction to Vera's goals. Vera wanted to slap him when he cried, but she didn't. Hadn't. She wanted to walk away, which she did as often as she could, but whenever she left the mewling baby in Trace's arms and shut the door to her study behind her, she was overcome with a sense of guilt. "Bad Mommy" reverberated in her head, and she was unable to put even a comma down on the page. All she could do was hold her head in her hands and rage. Post-partum depression, the doctor called it as he prescribed Prozac and exercise to get her back on track. That seemed to be working, sort of. She had run enough every day since (except when she was so pregnant that she could barely move) to be in training for the Boston Marathon, and she felt great tenderness for all her children, though she still resented how her aspirations had been stifled because of all these births. Still, Trace had wanted a big family. Having grown up as an only child, he had no idea what it meant to be surrounded by siblings and having to claw for attention every step of the way.

As she thought of Trace, something stirred inside her. They hadn't had sex for a very long time, and now she wondered why. Trace was a handsome man, a sexy man, and they had enjoyed many times together, sometimes in the most exotic ways. Just thinking about him brought Vera to her feet and heading toward the bedroom. Suddenly, she was overcome with desire. As she tucked herself in to the bed next to him, she reached down and felt to see if he was feeling stirrings too. Sure enough, his member was hard, and when she took it in her hand and began to stroke him, he woke.

"Well, hello, Sweetheart. Long time no see," he smiled. Vera reached up and pressed her lips against his, then climbed on top of him as she clumsily disrobed. Soon they were rocking and sliding, she the cowgirl on the mechanical bull, waving her hat in the air and yelling "Yipee!" When they were done, Trace propped his head up on his palm and brushed loose strands of Vera's hair from her face. "So where did that come from? Not that I'm complaining."

"Just felt like it, I guess," was Vera's reply. "I think I've turned a corner. I'm getting better."

Trace leaned over and kissed her forehead. "Glad to hear it. Welcome back." Then, he turned over and went back to sleep. Vera was wide awake, and whatever attraction she had momentarily felt for Trace was gone and now she was irritated by his snoring, his very presence. She wondered for a moment if there was something wrong with her. She certainly felt as if she was losing her mind. She imagined herself in a gladiator ring, being drawn through the dirt by a rope at the back of the chariot. Whatever was going through her head hurt, physically hurt. She lamented that working the 12 Steps and staying sober, taking Prozac and exercising daily were not enough. What else was she to do? Put one foot in front of the other ….

In the morning, her body was tired but her mind kept telling her to push on, push on. So she dutifully prepared the kids for school: Parker, 8, was in the 4th grade, in the same school as Jennifer, 6, in the 2nd and Cole, 4, in kindergarten. Normally, she would drive the kids to school, which was a little over a mile away. But today she insisted that they walk, while she pushed Rose in the baby jogger. Amidst cries of "It's too far" and "we'll be late" and "I'll get sweaty," she held firm as Trace watched her, sipping his coffee, and saying nothing.

"But Daddy!" Jennifer cried, flinging her arms around her father for support.

"Listen to your mother," he said, giving his favorite girl a kiss, then patting her on her bottom as Vera held the front door to escort them out. "You sure you want to do this?" he asked his wife quietly.

"It's not a big deal. It's a mile, for Christ sakes," she said irritably. To which Trace just held his hands up in defeat. "Last night was great," he whispered and winked.

With Vera directing a forced march from the rear, the trip only took about 20 minutes. Once school was in sight, Parker took off running down the hill with Cole, whose little backpack wobbled and slid on his back, beside him. "Hold Cole's hand," Vera yelled at the two boys who crossed the crosswalk together and disappeared into the building. Jennifer was standing very still by Vera's side.

"Go on, then, "Vera said, giving Jennifer a gentle nudge, but Jennifer didn't move.

"Look," the little girl said and held up her arms. Big, dark u-shaped stains marked her dress. "I can't go to school like this."

"Yes, you can. They will dry," Vera said firmly.

"But, Mom," Jennifer said, her voice choked and tears beginning to fall. "All the kids will laugh at me." Vera looked at her young daughter who looked so much like herself. Fleeting memories of elementary school in Iowa where the kids could be so brutal crossed her mind. She remembered being teased for her clothes and her awkward shyness. They called her "retard" and threw handfuls of dust, except Peaches, her best friend. Vera never meant to inflict the same horrors on her own child. Squatting down, she took some Kleenex out of the diaper bag that she'd brought for Rose.

"Here," she said, "put these under your armpits. It'll soak up the moisture in no time." Vera watched as her little girl stuffed the tissues into her dress. Then, Jennifer opened her arms wide and gave her mother a big hug. "Thanks, Mom." Then, she skipped off lightly down the hill, crossed the walk, and gave her mother a big wave as she went in the door to the school. *Why do I want to cry?* Vera thought to herself, then quickly shoved that thought out of her mind and ran off down the road, pushing the Baby Jogger as she steamed forward.

It was a beautiful autumn day, but Vera saw none of the bright yellow, orange, and scarlet leaves. She was oblivious to the crisp autumn air that seemed to smell of apples and cinnamon as though everyone had a fresh pie in their kitchen window. She didn't notice the other joggers or walkers or even strollers on the street, or the man with a pipe taking his black Newfoundland for a walk on a red leash. Everything was lost on Vera who was in her own head, caught up in an all too real fantasy that she was running the Boston Marathon, and winning. She heard the crowds cheering her on. She saw old friends and strangers waving banners that bore her name. She could feel the breeze on her face and the ache in her muscles. She knew she was only a few miles from the finish and that she would make record time. Closing her eyes, she could taste the victory; she would be in the papers and on the news. They would put her picture on the cover of *Sports Illustrated* and *Time*. Inches away. Seconds away. And then she heard the screech of brakes and a loud horn and when she looked up she saw that she had almost hurled herself and her baby into on-coming traffic. But the vision was so real. She could have sworn she was there.

"What's the matter with you, lady? You trying to kill yourself and your kid?" yelled the driver of the black Camaro who almost hit her. Vera didn't have an answer to that question. She honestly didn't know. Part of her wanted to laugh it off and attribute it to what she liked to call her "Walter Mitty" syndrome. But another part of her knew that this was something way different. This wasn't just imagination or creativity, this was a firm belief that she was there and that she had powers unlike any she really possessed. Something was wrong. Very wrong. And Vera was scared. She turned around and took Rose, who somehow had managed to stay asleep during all of this, home.

A quiet morning pushing Rose on the swing in the backyard and raking up piles of leaves which she showered down on the giggling baby's head brought Vera back to a calm place. As the mother and child sat on the wooden bench in the corner of the yard, watching leaves fall from the trees and playing "Itsy Bitsy Spider" up Rose's velvet soft arms, the terrors of earlier in the day were lost. Once again, Vera felt like she was an in-control mom. She would pick up the kids at 3 in the van, make mac and cheese with broccoli for dinner, and possibly even bake an apple pie. Jennifer would love that, helping roll the crust and sprinkling on the sugar and cinnamon. As she sat there with the baby on her lap, her face turned toward the sun, Vera felt an almost unrecognizable peace, a peace which was broken by someone calling, "Hello! Miss, hello."

At first, she wasn't sure if she was just imagining it, so she ignored the voice. Until it called out to her again, "Hello! Miss? I'm with Limelight Plumbing. Your husband called." Then, Vera looked and saw a man standing by the back fence, wearing a pair of overalls and a baseball cap. To anyone else, he would have seemed an ordinary man, possibly bordering on ugly. With his protruding belly, his pock marked skin and cauliflower nose, he was not what any woman in her right mind would call handsome. But to Vera, he was a god. She did not know it yet, but she had been stricken with a disease that lied to her about everything. It told her that she was invincible, that she could do anything. It led her to the bedroom and told her that aging plumbers were specimens of their sex. It buffeted her emotions, tearing her from limb to limb and all the while concealing itself. When you have cancer, you know something's up because you don't feel well and you lose weight. With migraines, there's no denying the piercing pain and the vomiting it causes. But with this, this mental illness, the victim is kept in the dark until all hell breaks loose and bank accounts are ravaged, marriages are ruined, and children are left with one parent, or none at all. Meanwhile, Vera was struck like Titania in *A Midsummer's Night Dream*, led to believe that the ass is a prince and that she is deeply in love.

It was the baby's crying that jerked her from her reverie, and a call from the school. She had forgotten to pick the children. Vera, who honestly had no idea where the day had gone, hustled to retrieve her little ones, all the while telling herself that she was the World's Worst Mother and trying to make it up by taking them all for ice cream before returning home to cook pies, fix mac and cheese, and stave off the depression that had settled on her like a mantle.

When Trace walked in, he asked her, "How was your day?"

"Just peachy," she replied, but, honestly, she was scared. There was something going on with her that she felt was about to burst. She just couldn't name it, there were no words. When she leaned over to kiss her husband and hug him, he smelled of violets and roses. A warning flare went off in her head. She immediately imagined the worst—a young intern at the publishing house where he worked. Vera saw her in a tight, black Spandex mini dress and chunky boots, with a tattoo on her collarbone that said, "Bite me." And leather wrist cuffs studded in silver. Vera was sure that if she were to look in Trace's pockets, she would find black panties, size 000. Not wanting to confirm her suspicions, she walked away and put the babies in a bubble bath where they sang "Baby Beluga" and blew mounds of foam into one another's eyes.

"Good night, Mommy" they cried, their little arms which smelled of cherries and baby powder circling her neck.

Vera went upstairs and quietly searched through Trace's jacket pockets, where she found nothing but spare change and breath mints. Relentless, she searched his trousers, all empty. There was nothing. She went over to the hamper and pulled the shirt that Trace had worn that day out of the laundry. It reeked of perfume. Almost as though someone has sprayed it deliberately. She dropped it on the floor and put her hand over her mouth to keep from screaming. But her anger and fear and sadness would not be quelled and she marched downstairs with the shirt in hand and dropped it in Trace's lap as he watched "Magnum PI" on the TV.

"What the fuck is this!" she yelled.

"Quiet. You'll wake the kids. Let's go outside," he said, taking her by the arm and leading her out the front door.

It was cold outside and very dark, as the moon was only a sliver of white. The sky was mottled with stars. Vera shook both with the cold and anger. "Who the hell's is that?"

"It is nothing," Trace persisted.

"If it's nothing, why does it smell like a brothel? And who does that perfume belong to anyway?" she cried.

"Nothing. It's nothing. She's no one," Trace repeated.

Vera was infuriated that Trace was protecting her, that he wouldn't tell the truth. Because that left Vera to imagine the worst.

That this had been going on for some time, that he cared for this girl. That he would leave Vera and the kids for cheap perfume.

"You've got to tell me. You owe me that," she said quietly.

Trace sighed. "It was just a fling. You were so depressed and unavailable. I had needs …" he began. Vera started to move toward the house. She had heard all that she needed to hear. It was her fault. She had driven him into the arms of another woman. "Wait, Vera," Trace said. "Let's talk about this. Can we talk about this?" But there was nothing more to say.

An hour later, Trace found her in the bedroom, sitting on the bed, and holding a bottle of pills in her hands.

"Do you think if one Prozac helps with depression, a whole bottle will cure it?" she asked, looking up at him with tear-stained cheeks. Then, before he could snatch the bottle out of her hand, Vera tossed the contents of the bottle down her throat and washed it down with water. Trace looked at her, dumb founded.

"You dumb, selfish bitch," he said as he dialed 911.

The next thing she knew, Vera was in the locked ward of the local recovery center, wearing white cloth pajamas and sporting paper slippers on her feet. She vaguely remembered the events that had brought her here. The day of crazy thoughts and actions, the explosive reaction to Trace's affair, but she still didn't understand why. Why she was thinking such thoughts and reacting such a way. Maybe she was just crazy and that was the whole explanation. But, no, she had for most of her life been reliable and productive, except for her drinking years. But at least for the past seven years she had been good. Good. Did being in this institution make her bad? She felt the life seep out of her onto the gray concrete floor. She knew if she stayed here long, painting chunky ceramic figures and eating with plastic spoons, she would lose her desire to live altogether. She wanted nothing more than to hug her children who stood on the other side of the glass waving weakly and wiping away tears.

As it turned out, Vera was released in a week, on the condition that she meet with a psychiatrist who could evaluate her condition and monitor her recovery. She was introduced to Dr. Imogene
Lasiter, an attractive, middle-aged woman with a kind smile and an
even keener ability to perceive and diagnose mental disorders. After
meeting for an hour with Vera, and asking a barrage of questions,
Imogene took off her horn-rimmed glasses, leaned back in her red
leather chair, and folded her hands across her taut stomach.

"It seems very clear to me that you have been misdiagnosed for
many years. In my opinion, you are a classic example of bipolar disorder. Now we begin the search to find the medication that will give
you relief from your terrible disease."

Vera didn't know what to say. She didn't know what bipolar disorder was, but when Dr. Lasiter restated the symptoms for her, Vera
could only nod her head. Just as she had felt when someone identi-
fied her alcoholism, she was relieved, and a little sad. She heard the
knolling of the bells, the straight jacket pulled a little tighter. Maybe,
just maybe, she hoped, this would require just a small amount of
daily vigilance to produce a better life in the long run. Honestly?
Vera had no idea what she was getting in for. She just knew that, for
now, the chariot had come to a stop, the horses no longer galloped
wildly away, and she felt a prairie wind moving across her mind. She
would take that vast silence any day.

LADY DI

It was a cool morning on Martha's Vineyard, the last day of August 1997, and a fog had rolled in overnight. Virginia sat at a glass table in the sunroom of the house they had rented for the month, wearing white silk pajama shorts and a red silk camisole, smoking a cigarette and nursing a mug of hot coffee while she fastened the last pieces onto a jigsaw puzzle of Hieronymus Bosch's *Garden of Earthly Delights* that she had been working on since they arrived.

They had come to Martha's Vineyard for three reasons: she needed to get out of the Texas heat, which was literally starting to drive her mad. More importantly, the president and his family were vacationing on the island at the same time, and she had visions that they would be invited for a drink or a swim. Neither had happened. The third reason, well there really was no distinct third, just that she wanted to flee something. The lover who had abandoned her. The cold tile floors of their mansion in Dallas. The echoes that reverberated through her very soul. She was forty years old, married to a man in his eighties who gave her everything she could possibly want in return for daily loving and really nothing more. He didn't ask for fidelity or even congeniality. He just wanted to see her pretty face across the table from him at meals and when she went down on him once a day.

Her face hadn't always looked like this. When she was younger, when she was first working for the airlines, when there were still stewardesses and free peanuts and working for the airline was seen as a sexy job, her face had been heart shaped with high cheekbones and heart shaped lips, with almond eyes that slanted slightly giving her an exotic look.

That was before her then husband, a businessman of Italian descent named Vincent Delgado, whom she had met on a hopper flight from Hartford to DC, during the Centennial. She was only 19. He took a broken bottle to her face, nearly blinding her in a drunken rage because he was convinced that she was seeing someone else on the side. He left her bleeding on the shag rug, and if her friend and colleague Dominique LaFleur had not come looking for her, she would surely have bled out and died.

Virginia remembered that night as if it was happening now. She remembered unlocking the door to the apartment and stepping inside. It was dark except for the light over the kitchen sink and the ghoulish yellow glare of the streetlights that seeped in through the windows. Vinnie was sitting in his favorite plaid recliner, dressed and ready for work in his stiff white shirt and black suit. A blunt burned in the ashtray on the wood table in front of him, which was littered with half a dozen beer bottles, all empty. He held another bottle in his hand.

"Well look who it is. Thought I wouldn't see you before I left for the office," he said evenly. "C'mere babe. Come sit on Papa's lap." He patted his knee for emphasis.

Virginia didn't want to go. She knew Vinny when he was this calm—the quiet before the storm. She knew that she had been with no one, come straight from her flight to home, only stopping to pick up a pack of cigarettes from the drug store, but she knew, too, that Vinny would believe what he wanted to believe. If he wanted to believe that Virginia had been servicing some pilot or dallying around with a passenger from the flight, he would believe that, and he would take it out on her as he had in the past. He had broken her ribs, dislocated her shoulder, kept her out of work for weeks at a time, complaining all the while that she wasn't bringing in any dough, all because, he said, he loved her. He had never loved her. She knew that now.

When he had come toward her with the empty bottle, which he broke on the counter, making it jagged and lethal, she knew that if she lived through this, she would leave him. She had to leave him. Enough is enough.

Later, as she was questioned about her injuries, she didn't tell the truth and give Vinnie up. She lied, saying that she had been attacked by a German Shepherd. She swore her friend to secrecy and wept whenever she looked at her mangled face in a mirror. But Virginia was not one to stew in self-pity. She did what she always did. She found a way to manipulate someone into giving her what she wanted. Wearing a dramatic black lace veil and widow's weeds, she marched herself into a number of plastic surgeon's offices. When the surgeon asked how he could help her, she did the great reveal, lifting the black lace up and baring her monstrous face. They were sympathetic until she confessed that she had no money for the procedure and asked that they do the work pro bono. Most refused. But one doctor, an Armenian, lit up when she approached him, practically salivating at the idea of taking this young woman's face which was a lattice work of stitches and puffed flesh, and piecing it into something beautiful.

"So, what you want?" he asked. "What look?" he said as he pulled out a huge book filled with photographs of beautiful people.

"You don't understand. I just want to look like me," Virginia replied.

"And you don't understand. There is no longer you. We must make you new."

Virginia stopped for a minute, considering what this meant for her. She had always liked her face, found it cute and perky, but now that face was to be replaced by something entirely different. What should she choose?

She looked through the book of faces, some celebrities some unknown, until she found one somewhere between Farrah Fawcett and Carrie Fisher. Here was a sultry blonde with bedroom eyes and luscious lips. She showed it to the doctor. He squinted a little as he looked from Virginia to the photograph and back again. Then, his face broke into a smile.

"Yes. Yes," he said. "Very good. Morgan Fairchild. A very good choice. The cheek bones line up, the rest we can, how you say? fudge. We will change the shape of the eyes and the color you can correct with contact lenses. This hair, of course, we will dye blonde." And so Ginger Book, as she now called herself, was born.

The airline had hired her back, even given her some of the more desirable routes, and on one of those flights she had met Larry Hawkins, a sixty-six-year-old oil tycoon whom she married at the age of twenty-six and she was still with today.

You would have thought that being married to a billionaire would be exhilarating—all those trips and fancy parties. The dresses. The jewelry. The shoes. But Ginger had found it all just a little bit tedious after a while. Though she loved the vast ranch that they lived on, she found that she was cold most of the time. Not physically cold, though there was that, but inwardly cold. She couldn't articulate it, but what she felt was a lack of connection. She lacked that feeling that she was a part of a relationship with someone.

If you had said that to her she would have laughed and dismissed you. She had plenty of relationships. As she sat on the top of the shining black grand piano and smoked a cigarette in a foot-long cigarette holder, she threw her head back and laughed at the absurdity. She had more than enough relationships with stable boys and bus boys and masseuses and married guests. And Larry. She knocked back booze and spread her legs and wondered why she felt so empty inside. What Ginger didn't understand was that she really had relationships with no one. She just used people to get what she wanted. She acted out of self-serving desires, but love? She loved no one, cared for no one, listened to no one. It was always about Ginger, all eyes on Ginger, her wants, her wishes, her desires, which left a hole bigger than a crater inside her.

As Ginger placed the last few pieces into the puzzle, she thought about the month they had spent on the Vineyard. It had been a quiet time, with no raucous parties and few houseguests. She had seen the president pass once in his caravan, flags waving, lights flashing, but she never got to shake his hand. Here they had rented a seven-bedroom, five-bath cottage with a vast kitchen, a private beach, a dock, and a boat, but not one of Larry's grown children—Terence, Tara, or Theresa—or his grandchildren had come to stay. Not one of Ginger's sisters or nieces and nephews had responded to the invitation. All the money they had couldn't buy them the friendship they desired.

"But when the lawyer is reading the will, see who shows up then," Ginger muttered to herself, spilling ashes on the puzzle as her cigarette jiggled from her lip.

Ginger put out her cigarette fiercely and walked out to the deck. The fog had lifted and the sun was breaking through. Gulls circled the still gray sky, screeching. Larry was sitting out on the deck in a dark green Adirondack chair, still in his white terry robe, the morning paper draped over his wizened legs as he cupped a mug of coffee in his hands. He was looking out over the beach and at the water beyond.

Down on the beach was a family of five, a tall, handsome man, a shorter blonde woman, and three small children. The man was kneeling in the sand with a darling little girl, probably two years old. Together, they were flying a kite, his large hands holding the reel while the toddler let the string slide through her fingers. She was both serious and amazed, squinting up at the kite so high in the sky, her little flowered bonnet framing her face like a flower.

Farther down the beach, the mother held the baby by two fingers as the little one lurched toward the water where her brother, maybe four years older, paddled an orange kayak on the inside of the waves. Brown as a berry with a shock of black hair, he was the spitting image of his father and showed spirit as he kept the boat right side up in the surf.

Ginger started to call out, "Hey, this is a private beach!" But Larry waved his hand toward her.

"Let them be. They mean no harm. Besides, I like to watch the kids."

Ginger sat down in a chair beside him. "You're too soft. You let people take advantage of you."

"You should know," Larry said, patting his wife's leg. "You should know."

Ginger wanted to argue, "What do you mean?" but she didn't have the fight in her. Besides why fight against something you know is true? Still, didn't he take advantage of her, too, using her pretty face and charm to sway clients at the dinner table, and wasn't he as guilty as she of abusing sex? She knew in her heart that servicing him daily was her way of maintaining the upper hand.

As she sat in her chair smoking a Camel, picking the small flecks of loose tobacco off her tongue, she pondered her life. Her marriage. Was this all a colossal mistake? Was marrying for money, for security worth it? What if he never died, or outlived her, would it have all been for naught?

Just then Jessie, the family servant they had brought with them from Dallas, raced across the lawn with her hands flapping and tears streaming down her face.

"She's gone! She's gone!" she wailed.

"Who's gone, Jessie? What is it?" Larry asked patiently while Ginger scowled, scrutinizing a chipped nail.

"Princess Diana. Princess Di. There was an accident. A terrible accident," she said, lifting her apron to blow her nose and wipe her eyes. "Those poor little boys. She was such a wonderful woman." Jessie spoke of Diana as though they were close friends, her hands trembling and tears streaming down her cheeks. "Such a wonderful woman. And so young. She should never have married that Charles. And that mistress of his, drove Diana mad. Poor girl."

As Jessie rambled on, Larry listened attentively while Ginger withered inside. Princess Diana, gone? It couldn't be. What was she thirty-five, thirty-six years old? So beautiful and loved. She was a Princess, Royalty for God's sake, nothing was supposed to happen to them.

Within seconds of lamenting Diana's death, Ginger had turned the spotlight back on herself. She wasn't much older than Diana, only four years, and probably just as rich if not richer. Like Diana, she had a loveless marriage based on convenience. Though Larry was no Prince Charles, committing adultery with some pie-faced cow, still Ginger felt abandoned and unloved. Larry's age was his mistress. It kept him from her because it was demanding and mean. The years had not been kind to him physically; his body was twisted, racked with pain, and he could barely walk, but mentally he was as sharp as a newly honed axe so that he knew just how disappointed Ginger was that he couldn't ravage her. The best he could do was stare and give her permission to fulfill her desires with other men, though it hurt his pride sorely to do so.

Like Diana, Ginger had taken on lovers. Multiple lovers. And she'd started to act carelessly, taking risks. Diana had taken risks and ended up dead in a car crash. Ginger didn't want to end up in a car crash, but she did want out of this life.

She wondered if she could convince Larry to give her a million dollars just to go away. Would he be willing to divorce her and settle? She knew she didn't deserve anything, except she really did for all those years of being his Baby Doll, but $1,000,000 could go a long way toward letting her buy a house, start a business, live on her own.

She had always loved fashion. She could see herself in a black pencil skirt with a stiff white blouse, collar turned up, long, red nails, and peek-a-boo black heels opening the door to her boutique on 5th Avenue in New York City. "Integrity," she would call it. Her motto: Dress with Integrity. Her clothes would attract celebrities and millionaires, and she could see herself on the cover of *Vogue* magazine. She would dress Emmy nominees and Oscar winners; she would achieve fame and fortune and men would flock to her ….

"Tinkerbell," Larry interrupted her thoughts, calling her by his pet name. "We need to get going. As fetching as you look in your silk pajamas, I suggest that you change into something more practical for the flight home."

Home. Ginger withered again. Reluctantly, she accepted her fantasy for what it was, a fantasy. She would never be free of this stifling life where she was kept and used, and used in return. She had all the things a woman could possibly dream of, but she lacked the essential ingredient for happiness, and that was gratitude. Virginia had long ago stopped saying "Thanks."

CIRCUS ACT

Of course, Victoria married the man with the knives, and in 1996 she gave birth to her second child, a little girl that they named Luna. Where Artie, Victoria's son, had coffee-colored skin and black Afro hair, Luna's complexion was the color of a peach petal in spring. Her eyes were as deep blue as lake water, and her hair sprung out in strawberry blonde curls, something neither of her dark-haired parents could explain. Victoria, who had mellowed into the gypsy life of the circus and was rather enjoying this episode of her life (which she lubricated with plum wine and ouzo) would sit for hours and tell you stories of her youngest who, though never having attended formal school, was smarter than anyone she had ever met. And wise beyond her years.

"She learned everything she needed to know right here," Victoria motioned to the tents and caravans around her. Anatomy she picked up from the fire eating man and the limber contortionists. She learned to add, subtract, multiply, and divide when she helped out at the gate, taking money and balancing the books. She loves the science behind knife throwing and the art of telling fortunes. She couldn't have had a better school," Victoria said, justifying the way in which she brought up her baby because she had nothing else to offer.

Eventually, Luna cultivated her own act, riding a tiny bike across a taut wire while holding a rose in her teeth. (Victoria's suggestion) At the end of her trek, she would toss the rose into the audience as if it was a wedding bouquet, and then bow. Victoria's favorite part? The thunderous applause which Victoria had never known in her childhood, neither literally nor figuratively.

When Luna reached the age of 13, Victoria took them from the circus and divorced husband 3 because, as she said, it was time for them to settle down. In truth, Victoria's drinking had escalated to the point that she shook uncontrollably. So now, when she saw the knives torpedoing toward her, she feared for her life.

ALL YOU NEED IS LOVE

Vera stood on the wide front porch of their Victorian home in Cambridge, Massachusetts, watching her four children walk down the street to the bus stop. The scene reminded her of her own childhood, making the mile-long trek from the farmhouse to the school bus, fighting with Violet all the way while Victoria remained aloof, and Ronnie just kept things under control. But today was no dark Iowa winter morning. Today, the sky was true blue and cloudless and the sun, no doubt, would burn off the chill by 10 a.m.

Vera waited for her children to disappear, fourteen-year-old Parker holding eight-year-old Rose's hand, which made Vera smile. How far life had come, Vera thought. She was light years away from being like either her father or her mother. How different her children were from she and her sisters. Her sisters with whom she had had little contact over the years since Vern and Valley died. It bothered her a little, knowing as she did that to maintain her sobriety she needed to make amends. But how do you make amends to people who don't want to forgive you? People said: It's not about them forgiving you. It's about you forgiving yourself. Just do the next right thing. Send birthday cards and Christmas wishes. Keep the channels open. The time will come if it is meant to.

The children had totally vanished down the street. It was time to work while she could, so Vera went back inside, poured herself a mug of coffee, leaving the breakfast dishes in the sink, and went to her study. In 1994, when Cole was born, she left the University Press and began to work from home, still editing manuscripts, a job she was good at in a situation which suited her. Trace had recently left the publishing business and opened a boutique literary agency with a fellow from work. His success made her opportunity possible.

It was a little after 7:30 a.m. and she was ready to settle in with her current project, a murder mystery about a woman who is complacent in her life, apathetic about her existence, until she finds herself framed for a murder she could never commit and spends the course of the book running from the authorities while seeking out evidence to prove that she is not guilty of the crime.

Vera had chosen to accept this job because it was a stretch for her. It required a lot of research and creativity. She, like the protagonist in the book, had started to take her life for granted. Vera was 46 years old, 22 years sober, married to the same man for 16 years, with four children ages 14, 12, 10, and 8. You do the math. Life was all about healthy snacks and folding laundry. Trace had encouraged her to move from the routine of her 8 to 4 job, and now she worked at home editing books and raising kids. She should have felt fulfilled but, instead, she just felt a little empty. The novels weren't fulfilling. She told herself that she should be writing her own. The kids were grown or growing. She saw little purpose in her life.

The phone rang at 8:50 a.m. At first, she wasn't going to answer it. This was her writing time, but seeing as she hadn't yet gotten started, stewing as she was in self-pity, and also seeing that it was her friend of twelve years, Adele Entermeyer, she answered the call.

"Oh my God!" Adele screamed into the phone. "Turn on the TV! Quick! The Twin Towers have been hit!"

Vera had no idea what Adele was screaming about but she diligently turned on the television and there she saw footage of a plane driving into the North Tower. At first sight, it didn't seem real or even possible. Were the pilots drunk or sleeping? As she watched the replay of the giant plane almost lazily shoveling into the North Tower, the footage changed as, at 9:03, a second plane crashed into the South Tower. Then, it dawned on her, this was no freak accident. This was intended, purposeful, and then she was gripped with fear and she shook as she saw the towers begin to crumble and she saw what looked like small black packages falling from the windows. Nausea overcame her, and she puked in a trash bin, realizing that those were bodies, people hurling themselves to a certain death. Later, witnesses would recall the sound of the bodies hitting the pavement as they fell from the sky. The worst kind of plague, a terrible waste of human life. Suddenly, Vera felt the overwhelming need to see her children, to make sure that they were alright. She hung up on Adele and called, first, the elementary school where Cole and Rose were fifth and third graders, respectively, but there was no answer only a busy signal. So she tried again and again, but the only response was the insistent beep. With her heart racing and her face flushed with anxiety, she was sure that she could just slip in between other frantic parents, if she just kept calling and praying, but to no avail. The junior high and high school were the same.

As she watched the images of the thunderous, thick black and gray smoke, and the faces of terrified victims coated in ash, like zombies, running from the catastrophe as those centuries ago might have run and cried in Pompeii, panic gripped her. What was next? Where were her children? Were her babies all right? Where was Trace?

Then, news of the plane crashing into the Pentagon emerged. And shots of a fourth plane en route to Washington, DC, taken down by passengers in a field in Pennsylvania. The world had gone mad. Surely Boston was next. Her home.

Wiping tears from her cheeks, Vera called Trace. Mercifully, he answered.

"Where are you?" she cried. "I'm so scared!"

"It's ok. I've got the kids. We're coming home. It's all right. Everything's all right."

Vera breathed a sigh of relief that her children were safe, but she knew that everything was not all right. Everything would be different from here on in. Nothing would ever be the same. Ever. Again.

That evening the house was subdued. Trace ran out to the store to get milk, bread, water, batteries and anything else he could lay his hands on in case this tragedy escalated into World War III. The children, led by her oldest son, Parker, played board games, Parcheesi and Monopoly. Picking that game now felt macabre to Vera but the younger children liked the little red and green plastic houses and the metal tokens and colored money, and it kept them busy for a long time. Dinner, when she made it, was simple. Grilled cheese sandwiches and tomato soup, made more to comfort Vera than anyone else, her heart was so heavy with worry and grief. As she sat in the biggest, coziest chair that they had, clutching her mug of tea in her hands, Rose got up from where she was sitting on the floor and came over to her mother. She stood in front of her and then climbed up into her mother's lap, taking Vera's face into both her hands.

"Close your eyes, Mama," Rose instructed. Vera closed her eyes and Rose, sweet little Rose, kissed first one eyelid and then the other. "You can open your eyes now, Mama," she said, and Vera opened her eyes to see her beautiful, blue-eyed daughter gazing at her. "It's going to be OK, Mama. God's got this." Then, she climbed down and went back to the game.

"God's got this," Vera smiled, remembering how Viveca used to say that long ago. And looked what happened to Viveca. And look what happened today? Vera believed in a God that cared for her, for everyone, but how did that jive with the day's events? Hundreds of lives lost, thousands maybe. The only answer that made sense was that God didn't do this. Bad people did. Evil people making evil choices. God still shone through in valiant firefighters, and intrepid passengers who gave their lives, in all the rescue workers and normal people who sent prayers and tears and relief as it was needed.

Vera determined that she would not pull a Valley. She would not bemoan the state of the world and give up hope. She would not pick up a drink to wash the fear and sorrow away. She would turn this situation over to God and ask for guidance. How could she help heal the wounds? What was she supposed to do?

An unexpected answer came: find your sisters. Vera would rather have done anything else—brought meals to displaced people at shelters, adopted abandoned lizards and snakes, held a prayer vigil in Faneuil Hall. But that was not what she was called to do. Her instructions were clear. Find your sisters.

The next day she started with Victoria, whom she hadn't spoken to for decades, not since she had joined the circus. At first there was no answer, but when Victoria finally picked up, all Vera could hear was commotion, like a crowd at a football game, and heavy machinery and sirens. It was all so loud that she could barely hear her oldest sister speak.

"Victoria! Victoria," she yelled into the phone.

"Vera?"

"I can barely hear you."

"I'm in the City. It's chaos here."

"The City? New York City?"

"Yes."

"Are you OK? It *sounds* like chaos there."

"It is. But I'm at an AA meeting."

"You are?" Vera said, startled by the news.

"I have a year sober today. Hell of an anniversary date. I'm living with some other women in the program."

Vera was dumbfounded. Victoria was a year sober, living with other sober women. Vera didn't know what to say except, "Congratulations!" Then, she asked, "How is it there?"

"It's insane. You wouldn't believe it, Vera, there's so much smoke and ash. It's worse than a war zone."

It is a war zone, Vera thought. "How is Artie?" she asked, suddenly remembering her 33-year-old nephew.

"He lives in Seattle. Has a nice wife and two kids. He's done well for himself in the computer business, nothing that I understand. Luna is living here with me."

"Luna? Is she one of your granddaughters?" Vera asked.

"Oh no," Victoria laughed. "She's my 15-year-old daughter. I guess you didn't know that I was pregnant when Valley and Vern died."

"Oh my God ..." was all that Vera could manage.

"I know. It's a long story. But the meeting is about to start. Got to go."

"Of course. Congratulations, again. We'll talk soon."

Vera hung up, astounded. How could she have not known that Victoria was pregnant? How could the years have gone by without a word? Her sister probably had no idea that Vera had married Trace and borne four children of her own, had a career as an editor, and had amassed years of sobriety. Vera had kept her life a secret. Suddenly, she wanted to share, to be connected and included, to mend the severed ties.

When Vera called the number she had for Veronica, an unfamiliar voice answered the phone, evidently a receptionist at Valley View Veterinary Clinic. When Vera explained that she was looking for Veronica Book, that she was her younger sister, the voice suddenly became warmer and jumped in to a conversation.

"Vera?" she said. "I've heard a lot about you. You're a writer."

"In a way," Vera conceded. "And you are ...."

"Parker. I'm Ronnie's partner and wife."

Vera swallowed. She'd known Ronnie was gay, but to hear this woman say she was her sister's wife still sounded foreign to Vera, as liberal as she was. Which made Vera sad, because how was the world ever going to change if prejudices lived on. Very slowly, she heard Adele tell her. One attitude at a time.

"I didn't know. Congratulations," she offered and then asked, "Is Ronnie there? I'd like to speak with her."

Vera had totally forgotten to tell Parker that she had a Parker, too, named after Robert Parker, the author. She imagined that Ronnie's Parker had been named after Dorothy Parker, the witty female writer who made comments like, "If all the women at Dartmouth Winter Carnival were laid end to end, I wouldn't be a bit surprised."

"She's in New York City picking up a couple of retired NYPD police horses in Hell's Kitchen. Don't worry. I spoke to her. She's fine," Parker said.

"Horses?" Vera asked.

"For Rainbow Ranch," Parker told her.

Vera had no idea what Rainbow Ranch was, so Parker educated her, telling her that Rainbow Ranch was Ronnie's baby, a ranch for abused and retired horses to keep them out of glue factories and dog-food cans. Volunteers, who just enjoyed being around the big animals, helped maintain the place, mucking stalls, feeding, grooming, and just spending time with the animals. They paid a modest fee for the pleasure of doing a day's hard work. No one seemed to mind and it kept the ranch afloat.

"Sounds like right up Ronnie's alley," Vera laughed.

"The kids love it too," Parker added.

"Kids?" Vera couldn't help but echo.

"Yes. We adopted two little boys from South Korea about eight years ago. Peter and Yves. They are 10 and 8 now."

Again, Vera was astounded. How every one's lives had unfolded and progressed while she was so busy living her own! How had it happened? She knew, immediately, what was missing: a hub. A mother ship to keep the fleet together. Since Valley's death, they had all flown off like puffs from a milkweed pod, landing in different directions. Now through this tragedy they were being called together. People all over the country, and the world were being called together. Great good was coming out of great evil. If only it could remain.

She thought of her children. All those years Parker and Cole had had boy cousins from China that they never knew existed. Vera kicked herself for keeping her family so locked away from her sisters and their offspring. She had thought she was doing everyone a great service, protecting her sober family from the sordid, dysfunctional family of her youth, but she had been wrong. It wasn't fair and now, if they got together, it would be awkward making up for lost time. But get together she resolved they would. If nothing else had come out of the devastation that was 9/11, she had gained a firm resolve to reconnect with family. Life was too short, too fragile to waste it away on petty quarrels and unpleasant memories.

As it turned out, Violet and Virginia were both in New York City, too, at the time of the attacks. Violet, whose career as a children's book author frequently took her into classrooms with the kids, was at the Little Red Schoolhouse on Bleecker Street, promoting her most recent publication, a book way ahead of its time on transgender issues, titled *When I Look in the Mirror, Why Don't I See Me?* The LRS, being a radically progressive outfit, welcomed such discussion, but, alas, the reading never took place as the smoke and ash filled the vents and poured into the classrooms. The children and staff had to be evacuated lest they die of asphyxiation. Violet poured her big heart into comforting the terrified children who wailed, wanting only to know the comfort of their parents' arms. Some would never know that comfort again.

Virginia, meanwhile, had come to the city with Larry to do a little pre-season shopping while he made deals with men in dark rooms. Or so she liked to think. For her, it was an excuse to get away from the tedium of home and to spend money. When the planes hit the towers, she was still sleeping on vanilla-colored silk sheets, in one of the suites at the Plaza Hotel, her quilted eye mask firmly in place, snoring slightly.

Larry, who had risen earlier, was fully shaved, showered, dressed and watching the television when he saw the first plane fly straight into the North Tower. He couldn't believe his eyes, listened for a report of pilot error, but when he watched the second plane fly into the South Tower, it shook him so much that he stood abruptly and knocked his chair out from under him where it landed with a loud thump on the floor.

"Oh honestly! Can't you ...." Ginger began.

"Get up!" Larry shouted. "There's been an attack."

For once Ginger listened and stood by Larry watching the replay on the screen, one hand covering her mouth while the other clutched her robe together. "Are we going to be all right?" she asked selfishly.

"It's not us I'm worried about," Larry replied grimly. "It's them," he said pointing to the screen which caught images of people running from the mouth of the smoke, on fire, and little children surrounded by chaos, crying as ash-covered firefighters carried limp bodies from the debris, laid them down on the street, and ran back in for more.

Ginger knew the shopping trip was off. She listened as Larry made one important phone call after another, trying to ascertain how he could be of help. While he couldn't do anything physically, he could throw money, lots of money, at the situation and he was entirely ready to do so. His advisors told him, let it settle to see where was the greatest need, but he was already setting up Trusts Funds for the Orphans of those lost in the disaster and working with the Emergency Relief Coordinators to make sure that they had supplies.

Ginger knew the greatest need. She saw it there on the screen, the crying children, terrified and alone. She decided that she would use the money she might have spent on new fall shoes, clothes, and tickets to shows on helping the children. "I want to go to FAO Schwartz. Now," she told Larry.

"Whatever for?" Larry asked.

"To buy the children stuffed animals," she stated, as if it was the obvious thing to do. "They are scared and alone. They need something to hold on to."

"That's a sweet idea, Tinkerbell," he humored her, "but there are more pressing needs."

Ginger stood there and, literally, stamped her feet. "Why don't you ever think my ideas are good?" she cried like a petulant child.

"I think your ideas are good," he said gently. "Just not now. Now they need to be moved to a safe place and bathed and fed. We need to find their parents, dead or alive, and relatives who can care for them. They are in shock. Their lives may have changed forever. If you think you can help with that, have at it."

Ginger turned on her heels and marched over to the bedside table, took out a pack of cigarettes and lit up.

"I thought it was a good idea," she muttered under her breath. "No one appreciates me."

By the end of the second evening after the attack, Vera had contacted all her sisters. She had discovered that she was an aunt to a niece and three nephews she had never met. Parker and Cole were eager to meet their boy cousins while Rose complained that the girl cousin was too old. Vera had spent quality time with her children while schools were closed, baking chocolate chip cookies and watching DVDs, and after the kids were tucked in, she and Trace had intimate time together, carrying on serious conversations about the future in hushed tones, kissing, making love, treasuring the present. Which was all they really had.

To give the children a purpose, to help them feel useful in a helpless situation, to calm them all down, closets were scoured for decent hand-me-downs and bags full of clothes, shoes, books, and toys were delivered to the church. Parker and Cole revived the old Philadelphia Flyer, which they took around the neighborhood soliciting canned goods to go to the American Red Cross. People, strangers, were nicer to one another in the streets and shops. We felt more unified as a community, a town, a country. Great evil had given rise to greater good.

Sadly, it wouldn't stay that way for long. Soon, the haters came with their bigotry and their profiling and their guns. Innocent Muslim families, long residents of the USA, were targeted and harassed, physically and emotionally abused. There would arise, as a result of the attacks, a pernicious strain of evil in our own country that fed on ignorance and false pride. Still, Vera focused on the good, on renewing old ties and sharing love. She made a plan that they would all be reunited at Trace's family's house in Vermont.

The wreckage of 9/11 was not cleared away that easily. Body by body, stone by stone the enormity of the tragedy was revealed. Stories came in from all over the country of loved ones they had lost, the final phone calls from the plummeting planes, the parting words as they leapt to sure death or suffocated in coils of smoke. To some it might seem clichéd, not to Vera, to her it was the very heart of life. No one calling from one of those planes going down or charging into the monstrous blanket of smoke ever said they wished they had spent more time making money or keeping long hours at work. They all, to the last one, wished that they had spent more time with their families and said "I Love You" so many more times. It was these last messages of love that brought Vera, sobbing, to her knees, praying that she still had time to make things right with her sisters. That had become the only thing that mattered, that and loving Trace and her four children. Rising, she wiped the tears from her cheeks, the snot from her nose. So many people had said it—Buddha, Jesus, a thousand poets—but no one said it better than The Beatles. All you need is love.

WHO RULES?

VERA WAS SITTING IN ONE OF THE WIDE, WHITE CHAIRS IN THEIR living room with Rose, now 7, on her lap and Cole, 9, on the rug in front of them. The grandfather clock chimed four, its deep, resonant bells reverberating through the house. Outside, day was settling into night and a soft showering of snow sifted down.

"Do you think the deers will come?" Rose asked, twirling a strand of her long, blonde hair as she posed her question.

"Deer," replied Vera, whose eyes remained fixed on the television set. "Now hush. She's on." "She" was Ellen Degeneres whose new show had aired in September and which was the highlight of Vera's otherwise drab and monotonous days. Ever since she had been diagnosed with bipolar disorder, she had been forced to cut back, way back, on her life. While the medicine had helped to dull the transition, she was still acutely aware of what she was missing. She missed the wild flights of fantasy that turned a simple tennis rally into a day at Wimbledon center court. She missed the illusion that when she walked into a room, people gasped at her beauty, as if she were Grace Kelly descending the stairs. She missed thinking that everything she did, wrote, said, or thought was golden. She missed the energy, the stamina, the do-it-all attitude she had when she was manic. What she did not miss was the near affairs, the running over people's emotions, the heavy price tag—both literal and figurative—that came with a manic episode, so she took care, great care, to treat her life with kid gloves, acknowledging how fragile and tenuous her happiness could be. And so to the burden of sobriety and all that entailed, and believe me, she had struggled mightily with not picking up a drink over the past five years, she added the responsibility of taking meds daily, eating right, sleeping right, exercising, blah, blah, blah.

If Vera weren't so scared, she would have thrown in the towel, but frankly, she couldn't imagine any other life that would sustain her. If she was honest with herself, she would acknowledge that it wasn't the kids who kept her on her new path, though she loved them dearly. It wasn't Trace, though they got along. It was fear that if she left this life there would be no other. She would simply die, and she wasn't ready to die yet.

Vera felt a tugging on her sleeve. "Are you going to dance, Mama? Ellen's dancing!" Rose cried and twisted and writhed in her purple leggings and embroidered pink swing top. Vera rose and took Rose's hands, twisting and smiling with her girl.

"C'mon, Cole. You going to join us?" Vera called to her younger son. At 9, he was on the verge of thinking this was all too un-cool, but Vera hoped maybe she could get one more dance out of him.

"Alright," he said, lifting himself slowly from the floor. Vera expected grumblings and protests, instead Cole dove right in with an electrifying display of moves that could only be described as unique. Spirals and spins, splits and somersaults, nothing was left out and Vera found herself gawking at this little boy who she barely recognized. When he finished, she clapped and went to hug him but he sat back down on the floor.

"Cole!" she cried. "Where did you learn how to do that?"

"School. Recess. Stanley," he replied tersely. Vera opened her mouth to reply, but Cole quieted her. "See, Mom, this is the movie I want to go to. It's the new Pixar. *Monster's Inc.*"

"I want to go," said Rose, who was sucking on strands of hair as she sat snugly on her mother's lap again.

"I'll tell you what," Vera said. "We'll all go. Maybe this weekend."

"Can't. It's not out until Christmas," Cole said knowingly.

"Then Christmas it is," Vera laughed. "Now, let's watch Ellen." But Vera was distracted by her own thoughts. Moments like this, she told herself, make it all worthwhile. Moments like this when she felt normal again, not like a cripple or a defective pear. Unfortunately, most of her days did not bring such happiness. Most days she got up, fed everyone breakfast and got them to school, and then came home, tried to work for an hour or two, but ended up back in bed where she slept until 2, quickly did the dishes, swept up Scholar's fur, and sprayed Clorox in the toilets to make it smell like she'd been cleaning. The older kids rode the bus and were home by 2:45, just before she left to pick up the little ones. Then, it was a quick stop at the grocery store, where Cole and Rose picked out cookies, back to Ellen, cook dinner, dishes, baths and bed.

Once as a child Vera had read a story called "The Routine of Happiness" about work horses that did the same thing over and over and were very content. But were they really? It was said that the definition of insanity is "doing the same thing over and over again and expecting different results." Somewhere in the middle of those two extremes was where she lived. She knew that she needed regularity, simplicity, in her life, but the way she was living was going to kill her. She needed to feel useful.

"But you are useful," Trace said to her as they talked about her concerns in front of a blazing fire. "You are bringing up our four kids. You cook. You clean. You edit books for people. You take care of me …." Vera wanted to roar.

"Don't you see it? Don't you get it? I'm taking care of everyone but myself!" Vera cried.

"But you are taking care of yourself," Trace said, baffled by her outburst. "You're taking your meds, going to the doctor, exercising …."

"That's all hygiene, mental hygiene, like getting your teeth cleaned regularly. That doesn't feed my soul," Vera interrupted. Trace took a long breath in and sighed.

"And just what would feed your soul?" he asked.

"I don't know," she cried. "It's like that line from the Randy Newman song, 'give me reason to live.'"

"You don't have a reason to live? We are not enough reason to live?" Trace said quietly.

"I don't know what you want me to say," Vera replied. "Do you have a reason to live?"

"Yes!" Trace jumped in. "You are my reason to live. And the kids. And the men I work with in AA. I get outside of myself and help other people, think a little less about myself and then I feel better. I feel useful. I believe that I am doing what God wants me to do on this earth. Am I a millionaire? No. Did I ever really make it as an author? No. But do I have enough, is it enough to keep me going? Yes. It's more than enough." Trace took a break and they sat there in silence. The fire cracked and hissed. Vera wasn't sure how she felt. There was part of her that admired Trace for being so put together and another part that wanted to kill him. For being so put together. She, on the other hand, had an emptiness in her heart which she knew enough to know that she could not fix. Only God could fix. But how could she trust a God who had taken so much from her—given her alcoholism and bipolar disorder, taken her parents and her sister, and deprived her of her writing. She needed help.

"Hello?" Adele answered with her throaty, smoker's voice as if it was the middle of the night. It was 10 a.m. and the sun was bouncing off the newly fallen snow, casting long, knife-like patches of light onto the kitchen floor. The prisms in the window splattered hundreds of drops of light all over the room, making it look like disco ball party. "Who is this? Do I know you?" she teased.

"I know. I know. At least I haven't picked up a drink," Vera said, dully.

"So. what's up?" Adele asked.

"It's me. I'm miserable."

"When was the last time you went to a meeting?" Adele asked. Vera couldn't remember her last meeting, but she wished Adele would shut up and let her speak. Without all the platitudes and pat answers. Why did everyone see everything in black and white? She was in a gray area and she needed help.

"I'm so mad," Vera began. "I'm so mad at God for taking everything away from me or, more realistically, for giving me things I didn't ask for." Adele just listened. Vera continued. "Like alcoholism and bipolar disorder."

"He also gave you sobriety and a plan to treat your mental disorder. Plus, he gave you four wonderful children, your husband, your dog. You have a beautiful home and vacations. Wonderful sisters. I'd say you've been very blessed."

"He took away my writing," Vera pouted.

"You've got that wrong, honey. He gave you an amazing talent but you have chosen not to use it. Out of laziness, fear, arrogance, I don't know what. But you're the one at fault there, not God," Adele asserted. Vera was quiet. No one had ever said that to her before, that she might be the cause for her writer's block, but now that Adele said it, she knew it might be true.

"Just supposing you're right. What do I do?" Vera asked.

"What are you doing this afternoon at 5:30?"

"I don't know. I've got the kids and dinner," Vera rationalized.

"Nonsense. What's the oldest boy, 13? Leave him some money and they can order pizza. You'll be back by 7 in time for baths and all that happy horseshit. I'll see you at 5. We'll get coffee." Adele instructed and then hung up. Vera looked at the phone, shook her head, and smiled. It was a beginning.

For the rest of the day, until the kids came home, Vera contemplated what Adele had shared. And Trace too. What made people feel useful? Goals. Parker's goal was to get into BU and play hockey and then go on to join the Bruins. Jennifer's goal was to join the US Women's soccer team. (Where had all these jocks come from in their family? Neither she nor Trace played competitive sports past high school. But maybe her children's aspirations would end there too.)

Cole's goal? He dreamed about making movies—as an actor, writer, or director, he didn't care. He thought it would be fun to do voice-overs on animated films and had even started making rudimentary videos of the silliest things, using his voice in a hundred different ways to tell a story. Rose just wanted to dance. She spent her youth in black leotards and pink tights doing *pleas* and *enjambment* across the tiles on the kitchen floor. Trace had achieved his goal of opening his own literary agency where he scouted new talent and represented great books.

But Vera was at home diminishing away, whimpering about her lost chances and challenging the choices God had made for her life. What kind of a God does that? She wanted to ask. To which Adele would reply, "There's no point in taking God's inventory." The better question to ask, the only question to ask, was "What are God's goals for me?" Vera knew that if she could just surrender to God's goals, her cup, which now looked half empty, would miraculously become half full.

FORGIVE OR FORGET

Men are such fools, so easily taken in and manipulated, and Trace Sunday was just like them all. With thirty-nine years of sobriety, *even with* thirty-nine years of sobriety, he had fallen for the play, like a redwood falling in the forest. *Timber!* Watch the bodies around him scramble to avoid disaster. Still, there would be collateral damage, lots of it, Vera thought to herself as she turned on the windshield wipers, which were ineffective against the torrential rain. The car was packed haphazardly with suitcases, computers, blankets, and pillows, anything she could stuff in the car spontaneously. She had put a Vermont address in her GPS and left the house filled with regret, but she had no choice. He had left her no choice but to leave this life that she had loved so dearly, this house where they had raised their babies and made a million memories. She felt, as she was leaving, that she was being slaughtered and she was not sure if it was the torrential rain or her weeping that was blocking her vision.

How could Trace have done this to her again? He justified it all so simply, as if he had had nothing to do with it, as if the affair had just slid into his life like a virus and taken him over. He called it being struck by compassion and brotherly love. Vera knew it for what it was: vanity and lust. When an older man, Trace was 63 now, "falls for" a girl in her 20s, what else can it be? Honestly, it was his ego being stroked by her neediness, her desire for a father figure wise beyond her years who could extricate her from the confusion of her youth. Hannah, who had joined his firm as an intern just months ago, didn't need a savior, she needed someone to boot her in the ass and tell her to grow up, to teach her how to restrain her wants and desires so that she could stop and think about what she was doing to other people, how she was harming other people just to satisfy a need she had inside.

Vera understood where Hannah was coming from. Long ago, in her drinking days, Vera's life had been all about personal gratification. She was locked and loaded to "ready, fire, aim," taking out marriages and destroying families in the process. But she had changed. She no longer flirted with other women's spouses, had never cheated on her own. She had become responsible, respectful, and reliable. Victoria commented, in a sober moment, that "that would have happened anyway as you matured, with or without AA."

Vera wasn't sure that she agreed. Growing old didn't necessarily mean growing kind or thoughtful or wise. Maybe that was true for some women, but men seemed to go backwards. Where once Trace had been the most dutiful, responsible husband and father, he now was chasing a piece of tail in the hopes of reliving his youth. Evidently sex with Vera was not enough. It was too familiar, flabby, known. Vera didn't stroke his ego the way that little Hannah evidently did, making him feel like the Big Man on Campus.

Vera told herself she didn't need Trace. She had saved money over the years and her job, though meager in pay, could support her needs. She didn't need anything that Trace could give her. But still, she wanted him. She wanted their memories, their experiences, their decades together that had bred loyalty, commitment, and understanding—until now. Now she was filled with anger and regret.

Yes, regret, she thought, wiping away the tears and turning down the speed of the windshield wipers to match the gentler, lazier rain.

She regretted that Trace had evidently needed Hannah more than his wife of twenty-nine years. Need Hannah? How could he possibly need Hannah? A young, not particularly attractive girl who was so mentally unstable as to be dangerous? How could he tell her in texts that he loved her, missed her, and would go through "this thing" with her? How could that land them in bed? Was his need really to help her understand her PTSD as he had come to understand his own, or was it the fact that he was needed by a weak woman, a woman who put him on a pedestal, unlike Vera who had long ago yanked him down, taken his hand, and insisted that they walk as partners, equals, side by side?

The squeaking of the wipers on the windshield told Vera that the rain had subsided. The sky was brightening slightly and shone like a gray pearl, luminous. Cars sped past her on the highway, hissing and spitting at speeds well above the limit, while Vera grazed along as if lost in a dream, unable to push her foot harder onto the pedal, to make the car surge forward, faster, toward her destination. She was tired, spent and tired. Her eyes, hot and swollen from so much crying, gazed out on the ribbon of road in front of her and she asked herself, *Vera, where are you going?"*

There is a truism: When I am having difficulty with someone else, there is something wrong with me. What was wrong with her? What part had she played in this fiasco?

It didn't take long for the answer to come, just a stop at a rest area and a trip to the gift shop for some gum. In the entrance was a bin full of trolls, all heaped up with happy, smiling faces. Vera remembered when she and Trace had been at a gift shop in Mystic Seaport not too many years before. He had wanted to buy her a small blue whale with a goofy smile painted on its face. But she had made him put it back because it wasn't exactly what she wanted. She had been looking for something more elegant, classier. His face, as she replaced it in the bin, reflected his disappointment. It was a small thing, but so telling.

Now Vera could see how she had always been that way with Trace. She had always brought stern judgment to the table. At first, it had been about asserting herself, trying to find out who she was and what she liked. That exercise had grown into a military maneuver with Vera as the General commanding the troops. She controlled everything from the gifts they gave the kids at Christmas to how they had sex. This was no mere opinion on Vera's part; this was the certainty that she had the better taste, the broader knowledge, and the wider appreciation for beauty which made her the obvious leader, leaving Trace in the dust. Very seldom, if ever, did she affirm him, so intent on affirming herself as she was, so they found themselves, two wounded soldiers, fighting over who was going to hold the tattered flag.

That Trace had responded to Hannah's overtures was not a surprise. She affirmed him. She made him feel The Man—appreciated, desired, and loved. Though Vera felt this way about Trace, she knew she had a funny way of showing it. The complacency in their marriage had made a chink in the dam through which the waters were starting to flow. She knew what she had to do if they were all going to keep from going under, and it wasn't a trip to Vermont. It was to reverse her course and speed home, if not to avert the disaster of Trace's affair then at least to pick up the pieces when he came to the realization that it was her lasagna he wanted to eat, and her lips he wanted to kiss before he pulled up the covers and fell happily, snoring, into a peaceful sleep.

Men are fools, Vera thought as she stepped out of her car onto the wet black driveway that was flecked with golden brown leaves. Men are fools, but women are fools too. We are all fools just trying to make our way in this life.

Later that morning, Vera was walking down the stairs in her plaid flannel pajama bottoms and a white T-shirt, towel drying her hair, having taken a long, hot shower trying to wash away all the bad feelings that were festering inside and to smooth out the hurt in her face and in her eyes. Trace was gone. She didn't know where he had gone, she could only imagine back to Hannah, and while that made Vera feel physically sick, she was resigned. There was nothing she could do but drink coffee, and wait. Wait for him to make the next move so that she knew what follow-up move she needed to make. Life is like a chess game, she thought, but then corrected herself. Life is no game. Games are meant to be fun. This was no fun. Life, she amended, is pain. You hurt, you hope, you hurt again, hope again, until you give up and die. She was not sure that she really believed that, but the way she felt now, it sounded good.

As she sat in the kitchen at the old farmhouse table, the black-and-white kitty clock shifted its eyes from left to right, counting the seconds passing with a flick of its tail. The sound of the ticking was ominous. Seconds of life passing away without certainty, or certainly they passed, just without resolution. Outside she saw a light snow had begun to fall. Nothing was sticking on the ground, of course, it was too early, only October, but the flakes fell and rested on the coral-colored leaves of the maple, damping the light that generally shone through the foliage and capping them with a new, quiet beauty.

Vera sipped her coffee, ran her fingers through her damp hair, and waited.

It wasn't long before the front door opened and Trace walked in to the kitchen, looking exhausted with his day-old stubble and messy hair, not at all his usual meticulously groomed self. She thought it made him look more vulnerable, sexy, though she couldn't believe she was having those thoughts now as he stood there, guilty as sin, the smell of his lover's perfume light on his clothes.

"It's done," he said quietly.

What's done? Vera wanted to know. We're done? She's done? You've filed for divorce? Vera wanted to ask, but nothing would come out of her mouth. Her eyes swam with tears as she contemplated all the possibilities.

"I just want you to know," he continued, "there was never anything there. She was just a lost kid looking for direction."

Vera wiped her nose with the back of her hand. She wasn't sure she believed this, but she wasn't going to say anything. Yet.

"There never was anything intimate," Trace went on. Vera coughed. "Well, all right there were a few intimate moments."

"How intimate?" Vera croaked.

"Is it really necessary?" Trace asked.

"It is if you want to preserve our marriage," Vera hissed back.

Trace walked over to the table where Vera was sitting, pulled out a chair, and sat down. Resting his elbows on the table, he ran his fingers through his hair.

"I can't see how this will help," he murmured.

"It will help me move from my exaggerated fantasies into a reality with which I can deal. And anyway, you are as sick as your secret."

Trace sighed. "She serviced me, several times."

"You mean she gave you blow jobs?" Vera stated matter-of-factly. "How many?"

"I don't know. Three. Maybe five. Seven."

Vera felt her face redden and her heart beat faster in her chest.

"But that doesn't count, really, does it?" Trace whined. "I mean it's not actually sex, is it?"

"You tell me," Vera said. "Did you have an orgasm?"

"Point taken," was his curt reply.

Now it was Vera's turn to make the move she didn't want to make. "Was there anything else?" she asked.

"Well," Trace sighed, "there was one time when we tried to have sex, you know. But nothing happened."

"What does that mean? Nothing happened? That you couldn't get it up? Couldn't get so far as taking your clothes off."

"Oh, no. We got naked, but I just couldn't do it. I kept seeing you and the kids. I just got dressed and left."

Vera knew that Trace was hoping she would say that counted for something, but she did not intend to give him that satisfaction. The truth was he had had oral sex with another woman, kissed her, gotten naked with her, and tried to do the dirty all the way. He just couldn't. She was pretty sure that he was telling the truth, the whole truth, that when he said it was over with Hannah, he meant it, but now what was she to do with all this information? She felt angry, self-righteously angry, and ashamed, embarrassed that her husband would seek "love" elsewhere. But she knew that she could not hold on to anger and resentment or she would surely drink again.

So, she did what any sober woman of integrity would do, she stepped out onto the snowy deck in her pajamas, light flakes dusting her arms and legs like lace, and cried. Then, she called her sponsor who listened and gave her sound advice, telling her to pray for Trace and for Hannah, that all manner of good things would come to them. As much as Vera hated to do that, really didn't want to do that, it felt hokey and fake, she prayed.

So that when Trace reemerged all clean shaven and handsome in his hunter-green V-neck cashmere sweater and form fitting jeans, she glided over to him as if propelled by grace, put her arms around his neck and kissed him.

"I forgive you," she said quietly. "Can you forgive me?"

"For what?" he asked, wrapping his arms around her waist.

"For driving you away. For giving you reason …."

Trace put his finger over her lips. "Let's just let this go."

Easy for Trace, Vera thought as they made their way toward the bedroom. But not easy for her. She knew that months, even years, of praying lay ahead and that the gremlin that had emerged from all of this was self-doubt. That feeling that she was not enough which could partner with self-pity, jealousy, anger, and fear, bringing down the whole house of cards. This was the game, then, not chess but Life dealing hands you didn't bank on, taking you down roads you'd been down before, daring you always to do better, be better, love more.

There really wasn't any alternative, Vera thought as she looked over at her husband lying in bed beside her, snoring. So best to forgive if not forget.

LUNA GETS MARRIED

CHERRY BLOSSOMS, PALE PINK, AND FROTHY ON THE TREES, WERE loosed by the wind and fell like snow, scattered on the gray sidewalks and granite benches in DC. Vera walked on the Mall, alone. She had come to see the cherry blossoms by herself, to recreate the moment that Vern asked Valley for her hand in marriage. It had been so many years since her parents died, longer than that since they loved each other; it felt like forever since she had known that kind of love. She had gone to Washington to wander in museums and fill her mind with images of wondrous things—Dorothy's ruby slippers, the Wright Brothers' aircraft, the Hope Diamond—anything but the ghosts that haunted her mind, the visions she saw of Hannah and Trace together, the heaping sorrow that lay on her chest like a wooly mammoth and threatened to suffocate her with every breath she tried to take. She left Trace at home almost as a test to see if he would be tempted to return to Hannah, if he would follow through, though she was pretty sure he wouldn't. But also, she didn't want him with her under the trees when she was thinking about her mother and father and how love destroyed them both.

Running her hands across the cold granite of the Vietnam War Memorial, she was reminded of boys she had known who had gone to, or escaped, the war. She wondered where Joe Cadwallader was now with his devilish grin and seductive ways. And Jacob—she couldn't even remember his name. She saw in her mind's eye the little cemetery in her hometown awash with small American flags, each representing a fallen hero. She used to know their names, many of them anyway. She used to go to school with them and to the drive-in. They used to smoke pot and kiss, and now they were gone. Long gone.

Viveca was gone too. She would never know the troubles that Vera was facing, the sorrow that her life seemed to have failed so miserably. Actually, Viveca would be the one to tell her to "buck up," put her faith in God, and trust that everything was going to be all right. Vera might have believed that years ago. She had spent decades turning her will over and seeking God's will instead, but somewhere something must have gone terribly wrong. Or else God was a cruel and arbitrary deity because here she was, surrounded by the most magnificent beauty, despairing over her parents' ruined marriage and her own.

Even saying that, she knew it wasn't true. She saw Jennifer and Rose dashing and darting down the Mall toward her, arms open wide, full of laughter and life and promise. "We thought we'd never find you!" Rose gushed as she gave her mother a huge hug.

"I never doubted it," Jennifer smiled, kissing her mother first on one cheek, then the other, European style.

"My girls," Vera whispered, wiping a tear from her eye.

"Oh, Mom, you can't cry! This is all good!" Rose laughed.

"This is me happy," Vera explained. "Tell me about your jobs. Isn't it just so ironic that you both ended up in DC?"

"DC is where it's happening Mom," Jennifer said.

"Are you happy at the State Department, Jen?"

"Very," Jen replied.

"What about you, Rose? How's that lobbying going?"

"Great! Tough. Frustrating. Great!"

"Oh dear," Vera sighed.

"Why the 'oh dear'?" the girls asked in unison.

"I just always thought you'd be off dancing someplace. You always were such twirly girls."

"That's what we do when we are not working," the girls laughed.

The women linked arms and walked three abreast, ignoring the sideways glances of other pedestrians on the Mall, plowing their way through.

"So, tell me, what's the scoop on Hillary Clinton? Do you really think she has a prayer?" Vera asked.

"Personally, I'm for Bernie," Jennifer said firmly.

"Me too," Rose agreed. "Hillary's past may catch up with her and bite her in the butt."

"We all have pasts, my dears, and they all do catch up with us. It's whether you learn from them or not that is the mark of a wise woman. I personally would like to see a woman in the White House as POTUS not FLOTUS. But enough politics. The election is a year and a half away and a lot can happen. Where shall we eat?"

As they sat at a little bistro tucked into a corner on a street Vera had never heard of before and would never find again without her daughters' assistance, Vera picked at her pistachio-pear salad and enjoyed the easy conversation between her two daughters as they talked about everything from conservation to Congressional hearings, Kate Spade to Kate the Duchess of Cambridge. Light and energy radiated from around them and Vera felt that she was in the presence of Joy. But Joy wasn't her primary mood. It was something more bittersweet. An aching in her heart that reminded her that however perfect this moment was, her life wasn't perfect at all. She wondered what life would be like without Trace.

"Mom? Are you okay? You look like you are going to cry," Rose broke in to her thoughts.

"It's nothing," Vera lied.

"Are you sure you are all right, Mom? I can get you some water …."

"I'm fine," Vera said brightly, patting the top of Rose's hand. Just then, Vera's phone chirped. She saw that it was a group text to each of her sisters from Victoria. "LUNA'S ENGAGED!!!" it read.

"Luna's engaged!" Vera exclaimed, glad that the channel had changed off her introspection, and was now dialed into something far more fun.

"Luna? Our cousin Luna?" Jennifer asked.

"Yes! She's been living with Arlo for quite some time. I guess they finally decided to tie the knot," Vera said.

"Isn't she old? Like really old?" Rose asked.

"She's 28. That's not old," Vera stated defensively.

"Where? When?" the girls chirped in unison.

Vera smiled. "Details to follow," she replied and lifted a forkful of greens to her mouth.

In fact, the wedding took place the following summer at a state park in Vermont. Luna and Arlo had been living in a cabin in the woods by the lake for seven years. They had seen wedding parties come and go, pretty brides standing by the water's shore in beautiful dresses while the background around them, this bowl of trees and mountains, changed like a kaleidoscope from vibrant green to orange and gold and scarlet to dark silhouettes of maples and ash to green again, a soft green that whispered the beginning of the cycle once more. One day in fall, as Luna and Arlo were taking their daily walk around the lake, calculating the growth of the band of white-capped mushrooms by the big pine and admiring the way in which the ferns blushed from green to pale yellow, Arlo had dropped to one knee, run his fingers through his curly shoulder-length hair, and cleared his throat. The woods were exquisitely still with only the breeze rustling through the colored leaves overhead and setting several golden teardrops falling gently to the ground. A solitary bird sang in the distance, its song trilling across the quiet like a silver bell. Luna thought that Arlo's shoelace had come untied until he reached for her hand and slipped a wide silver and amethyst ring on it, asking, "Luna, will you promise to live with me forever? Will you marry me?"

Luna, who generally held back her emotions, could not stop the tears from flowing. Years of suspicion that she would never know lasting happiness slipped away and she threw herself into Arlo's arms, knocking him down onto the forest floor that smelled like pine and dying leaves.

"Yes, oh yes!" she cried. "I thought you'd never ask!"

෨෦

They were married by the lake on a perfect late-summer day, the sky a flawless blue and a cool breeze giving just enough relief from a still-strong sun. Everyone had made provisions to be there, all the aunts and uncles, the cousins and friends. A mixed group of people it was, people of all ages, colors, religions, and nationalities congregated on the shore to watch Luna and Arlo exchange their humble, heartfelt vows. At the end of the ceremony, after the bride and groom had kissed, they stripped off their formal clothes. Off came the white lace wedding dress. Off came the vest and formal shirt and jeans. And there stood Luna and Arlo in their bathing suits, just married, as they raced towards the water hand in hand. Luna had neglected to take off her veil and it floated around them in a milky cloud as they held each other and kissed. The crowd went wild, whooping and clapping. Some brave souls stripped down and joined in, plunging into the icy waters. Vera stood on the shore, grinning, delighted by their spontaneity while Victoria, Mother of the Bride, elegant in a brown silk polka dot shirt dress, held her current husband's hand. He was the fourth and, hopefully, the last she said. "Jonas is my sober catch," she smiled and brought his hand to her lips, "the love of my life." Apparently, he had done her good, Vera noted, as Victoria was calm and serene for the first time that Vera could recall.

As Luna pulled on a pair of cowboy boots and started playing kick ball with some of the younger guests, Victoria shook her head declaring she had had nothing to do with this, while smiling, satisfied that this was just what she would have expected of Luna, her spirited child.

A picnic was spread out under the pavilions and everyone enjoyed simple fare, a potluck feast of simple salads, luscious fruit, and chicken grilled to perfection, and the most delicious seven-tier lemon cake with white chocolate frosting courtesy of a baker friend of the couple who had been waiting for this wedding for a long time.

Vera filled her plate and was on her way to sit at a picnic table with several of her sisters when she noticed Trace sitting alone on a bench overlooking the lake. She put her plate down and walked over to him.

"What are you thinking?" she asked. He shook his head.

"Nothing," he responded.

"Trace, please, tell me what you are thinking," she implored.

"Nothing. It's really nothing."

"Are you thinking about her?" Vera asked cautiously.

"Who?" he replied.

"Hannah," she said.

"God no!" he exclaimed, genuinely surprised. "Why would I be thinking about her? That's been over for years. Done. You've got to let that go, Vera."

"I'm ...." Vera started.

"Honestly? I'm thinking about moving up here."

"Really?" she said, her face brightening. "You'd move here?"

"Sure," he replied, "why not? The kids are grown and out on their own. We could move into my folks' house now that they're gone."

"I would love that," Vera said quietly. They could find new meetings, a new set of friends, away from the gossip and controversy surrounding their relationship. Away from Hannah. Was it possible to start again, to build a new life together? Didn't they say, "Wherever I go, I am there with me?" But she felt that if they lived somewhere new, made new memories, they could erase the smudge that was there in the past. She would not hold onto disappointment the way that Vern had. She would let go and move on, unless it happened again. Then, she would either kill him or leave. But that was not today's problem.

Trace took her hand and they sat there for a long time, looking out at the diamonds dancing on the lake. Behind them, little children waving bubble wands ran in the sun and dogs with festive collars caught Frisbees in midair. Couples too stepped on the grass to the music that was being piped in, and Arlo and Luna held on tight to each other, fastened to a new life.

"I'm sorry I hurt you. I truly am," Trace said. Vera turned her head to look at him.

"That's all I needed to hear," she said.

They kissed and while the events of the past didn't vanish, they were momentarily diminished and Vera felt hopeful that they could leave all the pain in the dust, that Life would do what Life does which is, if you're lucky, to heal all wounds with Love.

WITHOUT TRACE

A YEAR LATER, VERA SAT ON A COLD, BROWN PLASTIC CHAIR IN THE examination room of the oncologist's office at Mass General. She held her hands together tightly, in prayer. What had started as a routine check-up for Trace, who was suffering from some problems with urination, trouble maintaining an erection, and fatigue, all symptoms that both she and her husband had attributed to his advancing age, had turned into a series of MRIs and CAT scans and bone density tests. The result was this, Trace lying on the examination table in a washed out blue "nightgown" which revealed his weight loss. Another symptom. The doctor, all efficiency and concentration, listened to Trace's chest and his back. Then, he helped the weakened man up to sitting position.

"Why don't you get dressed, and I'll be right back," the doctor said, as he disappeared out the door and left the couple sitting under the sallow light, the hiss and hum of the fluorescents providing background music to their anxious thoughts.

"It's all going to be alright," Vera said lamely as she looked across at Trace, who had his head in his hands.

"We don't know that. It is going to be what it is," he said matter-of-factly, as he hopped down from the table and began to dress. Vera watched as her husband pulled on his too big clothes. Her heart felt explosive in her chest as it was flooded with emotion and thoughts. What if this was something really bad? What if they couldn't fix it? What if Trace died? Vera wiped away emerging tears and told herself not to be hysterical. But she couldn't imagine life without Trace. For all his shortcomings and bad behavior, he was still a good husband and father. He had been good for 30 years. She found herself bargaining with God, a useless activity, she knew, but if God would just keep Trace healthy, make him healthy, she promised to stop whining about the things she didn't have. A career as a published fiction writer. A house in Vermont looking out over the mountains. She stopped there because the doctor came back in the room, armed with films and files, sporting a happy smile on his face. Good news, Vera hoped. For several minutes, he chatted with them about their family. Grandkids. Vacations planned. The upcoming holidays. And then, like a magician, he swirled his black and red silk cloak and emerged on the other side all serious and morose.

"I'm afraid I have some bad news," he started, and the tears welled up in Vera's eyes again. Be strong, be strong for Trace, she told herself, but she didn't feel strong. She felt like she was being flushed down some spiritual drain and all her faith and hope were going with her. "Look here at these films," the doctor said, slapping the murky gray and white images up on the screen. "See this? This is your prostate. And this stuff, this is the cancer."

"Can't you just take it out?" Vera blurted.

"If only it were that easy," the doctor sighed. "Unfortunately, you have Stage 4 cancer which means that the cancer has spread into your lymph nodes and traveled to other parts of your body. It's incurable. We can try to arrest the spread by giving you chemotherapy, but you should be aware of the side effects. We'll be using docetaxel and prednisone"

Trace looked up from where he had been staring down into his lap. "How long?" he asked.

"Maybe five years," the doctor replied, "with the chemo. Let me put it this way: you should get your affairs in order." Vera's hand flew to her mouth. She couldn't believe what she was hearing. This was ridiculous. Just this morning they had been sitting on the deck in the sunshine, drinking tea and admiring the crimson leaves on the Japanese maples, and now, this?

"Thanks for that, doc, but I meant how long on the chemo?" Trace said, smiling weakly.

"I'm sorry. I misunderstood you," the doctor said, unfazed by his mistake. "Of course. Three weeks on, three weeks off. We'll follow that for a couple of months and see if there is any improvement."

It was almost too much to bear. In the background, she heard the doctor and Trace talking about starting chemotherapy later in the week, but mostly Vera's mind was filled with a thick fluff, like pillow stuffing, that was trying to absorb the onslaught of terror and grief that were overpowering her. It was selfish, she knew, after all, how must Trace be feeling? But it was the best that she could do.

The kids took the news of their father's illness with predictable responses. Parker, who had long since given up his dreams of being a professional hockey player and who was, instead, selling stocks and bonds, peeled through the contacts on his phone to see who, among his many friends and clients, might have helpful information to input into the situation. Jennifer, a data analyst at the State Department, surprised Vera by rattling off homeopathic remedies and other resources, anything to keep her father from losing his thick head of curly salt-and-pepper hair. Cole was quiet when he learned the news, but the next day a huge basket arrived from his home in California with healthy fruits, nuts, teas, and chocolates. Plus, a note that read: Dad, I'll be out as soon as I can. Thinking of you. Love, Cole. Rose just cried.

The cycle of chemo began with all the unpleasant side effects that came with it, the worst of which, for Trace who took pride in his looks, was losing his beautiful curly hair. The other side effects he managed to live with, the loss of appetite, fatigue. Nausea and diarrhea, they gave him something for and he dealt with that as it came.

Vera, meanwhile, turned all her attention toward being his caretaker. She bought special cookbooks which were filled with recipes for those with cancer, those undergoing chemotherapy and everything in between. They began juicing at least three times a day to give Trace the nutrients he needed but could otherwise not digest. She encouraged Trace to do a little exercise every day, if only a stroll around the garden, and to sit outside in the sun. She read Trace happy stories and rented comedies, trying to keep his spirits lifted. All this she did more for herself than her husband who was gradually disappearing inside himself, drawing closer to the golden gates that would welcome him home. The more reclusive Trace became, the sadder and more frightened Vera was until one day, he took her hands in his. It was a perfectly lovely day. The sun was shining and sparkled on the fresh coat of snow that had fallen the night before. In the high branches of the trees, the winter birds twittered. Peace.

"You know, dearest," Trace began, "We have had a wonderful life together." Vera nodded, tears, always those tears, welling up in her eyes. "I've made a few mistakes. We've both made a few mistakes. But I think we're good."

"We are," she managed to say.

"I'm good," he said. "I'm ready. But I can't go if I know you're not. So, listen, you'll be taken care of. There's plenty of money. My life insurance policy is huge …."

"Stop it!" Vera said, wiping the snot from her nose on her sleeve.

"I can't stop it, sweetheart. You know I can't. The house in Vermont that Mom and Dad left me, I've had it put in your name. My funeral arrangements are simple: cremate me, stick me in a can, and bury me in the garden in Vermont. That way, I'll be able to keep an eye on you. Make sure you're going to meetings. Taking your meds. Eating right," he smiled.

She reached over and hugged him, holding him close, tears streaming down her cheeks.

"Please don't go. I don't want you to go," she sobbed.

"We all have to go, darling. You know that. I've had a good run. I don't want to do this chemotherapy any more. It's time. Can you understand that? It's time," he said quietly. Vera nodded. She did. She understood. But she didn't like it and it didn't make it any better.

Three weeks later, Trace died, peacefully, in his sleep. Vera was there with him, half dozing, and she swore that when he took his last sweet breath a thread of sparkling light rose from his chest and disappeared through the ceiling. Vera was on her own.

NOT THE FINAL CHAPTER

WHILE TRACE WAS LIVING OUT HIS LAST DAYS, THE COUNTRY WAS frenzied over the on-coming election. Each party would have you believe the other candidate was the spawn of Satan. For Vera, who was already grieving her loss, politics mattered little. She had more pressing matters on her mind. But on November 9, 2016, when she and the rest of the Book sisters woke to read the news that Donald Trump had been elected President of the United States, Vera's heart sank.

Victoria, whose life had been changed at an early age by not being able to abort her unexpected child, felt a deep sadness for all the young women who would find themselves in that position. With no Planned Parenthood, no free birth control, and no access to safe abortions, there would be no choice for them and they would really be robbed of their choices.

Veronica, who had not slept all night but watched the nation turn a blood-curdling red, feared for her life and Parker's and for the lives of their friends. She contemplated running away to Canada or New Zealand, but what message would that give Peter and Yves? And what about her horses, the clinic, the life that they had built here? No, she would stay. They would stay. They would fight, if necessary, because weren't they citizens too?

Violet got a little bit hysterical, reminding Ben that in Nazi Germany it was the artists and the intellectuals who were thrown into concentration camps. Ben soothed her, telling her that though Trump blustered, he was no Adolf Hitler. His biggest fault was that he carelessly opened Pandora's Box, letting loose, hatred, ignorance, jealousy, and anger into the world. But, Ben reminded her, we haven't lost hope. She rests at the bottom of the box waiting for us to retrieve her.

Virginia voted Republican, simply stating that she "didn't like Hillary's politics." She lit a cigarette and stood at the massive living room window, looking at herself again.

Vera felt that she was on a down elevator going very fast. She was sick to her stomach and stunned. Did she really live in a country where the majority chose hate over love? How had that happened? She thought of Vern and Valley and so many others who had sacrificed so much in the fight against bigotry and hate. Vera felt herself beginning to charge into battle, holding the colors like Joan of Arc. But listening to the cries she read on the Internet — "Reject Trump!" "Stand Against Trump!" "Never Surrender!" scared her almost as much as the voices yelling "Hillary in Prison!" and "Down with Niggers and Gays!" They were all hysterical voices that, clashing, could bring no resolution, only bloodshed and death. For her, they brought a thirsty desire to escape back into the bottle. What Vera did instead was to walk out into the icy November air, stand under a wintry gray sky just shot through with deep red streaks of sunrise, and ask her parents, Kennett Jenkins, Viveca, Saint Lucy, the Mother Mary, Trace and Jesus Himself to intercede on the world's behalf, bring peace and wisdom. If they couldn't reach the politicians, could it reach as far as her heart so that she might be the most compassionate person she could be, loving God and all God's Creation in every breath.

GEM-TACTICS

VERA HAD TO GET AWAY. IT HAD BEEN TWO MONTHS SINCE TRACE died, and she had faced, every day, from her children, who called relentlessly, and from well-meaning friends who made offers of breakfast, lunch, and dinner, the same unanswerable question. "How are you doing? How do you feel?" She knew a woman who, like she, had lost her husband. Whenever Vera saw this woman, she wanted to scream "Alice! Get real!" because Alice would wander around giving and getting hugs, being resolute and shutdown. She was fine. It was fine. This was all in God's plan. Good for Alice, thought Vera as she sat across from her at a meeting shortly after Trace's death and Alice made a sad face at her, and wrung her eyes, lay her hands on her heart, and blew a kiss. The sign language of compassion, but it was enough to make Vera's skin crawl. She knew it wasn't Alice's fault. She was just empathizing. It was Vera who was off, and she needed to get away.

She needed, too, to get away from everything that was going on in the world. Daily phone calls from Rose lamenting every action the new administration was taking were more than Vera could bear. She wanted peace. She needed peace. She needed to be out of reach for a while so that she could adjust to her new life. Widow. The word cut such a wide hole in her heart. It left an enormous opening for the winds of change to blow through. Now, all she was feeling was emptiness and, looking closer, fear. What was she going to do with the rest of her life? She was 61 years old. Sure, she had plenty of money. There was no problem there. Materially, she was set. Physically, she was in good shape. But spiritually? She knew she needed a desert experience to allow the Universe to speak to her, guide her, spin her around, and set her feet going in the right direction. And so, despite all the worried and concerned voices that told her that it was a bad idea, she rented a cottage on the Outer Banks for a month. She'd be back in late March. Hopefully, winter would have left Massachusetts by then, though she had no expectations, and soon she'd be able to bury Trace in the garden in Vermont. She would plant a creamy, white Peace rose above his ashes, and over time, she'd watch it grow.

So off she went. The journey, monotonous and long, took two days. When she finally arrived at the cottage, she wondered if she had made a big mistake. There was no doubt that the location was beautiful. The cottage was just a stone's throw from the beach where the ocean roiled and reared, tossing white spray into the winter wind, and crashing as loud as cymbals on the sand. But the house? It was weathered and looked uncared for. She hoped she hadn't made a grave mistake. The look of the cottage from the outside reminded her of the frightening black and white sketches in an old copy of *Jane Eyre* she read as a child. Thoughts of mad women and murderers littered her head. *Don't be stupid*, Vera told herself. *You are the only mad woman here. The pictures were nice. Go inside.* She did.

The interior couldn't have been more different from the out. When she turned on the lights, she felt immediately as if she had just entered Smaug's cave as each room was painted the color of a precious jewel. The aquamarine living room led on the right to a galley kitchen that shone like peridots. The bathroom, a rich garnet, was attached to the bedroom, a deep amethyst purple. Vera was stunned by the vibrancy of the colors and a little uncertain how she felt about all this brilliance. Maybe she should have gone to their house in Vermont with its stark white walls and gleaming hardwood floors. For a moment, she considered reversing her steps, but then she hesitated. There was another room that she had not yet entered. She walked over and cautiously opened the door, a little frightened lest she suddenly be overcome with emerald or citrine. But when she opened the door, all she saw was white. Luminous white walls, a white desk, and shelves. The only color in the room was a big red leather desk chair which she immediately sat down on. Even through her heavy sheepskin coat she could feel how comfortable it was. As she ran her hands across the smooth, white desktop, she noticed a small frame with a poem inside. Given that there were no other pictures in the room, or decorations, Vera paid attention, picking it up and reading what it said: *We play at paste/til qualified for pearl/ then drop the paste/and deem ourself a fool/the shapes, though, were similar/and our new hands/learned gem-tactics/practicing sands.* Emily Dickinson.

Of course, gem-tactics, Vera thought as she contemplated the poem. That's what I'm doing here. Learning gem-tactics. But what did that mean?

As Vera unpacked the groceries she had bought on the way out, placing them in the small refrigerator, she thought about Trace. He would have loved it here, the sound of the ocean right outside the window, the cozy set up in the house. In fact, he was there with her, his ashes in the urn she brought down with her. She had thought about leaving him home, but she wasn't ready yet. And so, after she had put her clothes away and hung the towels in the bathroom, she buttoned herself up into her coat, pulled on some gloves, scarf and a hat, retrieved the urn and went out to walk on the beach.

February can be a cruel month and very cold. With the thirty-mile-an-hour wind and the bitter temperatures rising off the water and mixing in the air, Vera felt her teeth chattering and her eyes stung with tears. But she would not go back. Something was calling her to go on. Through squinting eyes, she saw someone coming in a distance. A fisherman with a pole and a white bucket. Hard to imagine anyone fishing on a day like this, thought Vera as she pulled her scarf tighter around her neck. But people do all sorts of crazy things when they love something. Or someone. She wasn't going to fool herself that she and Trace had had the perfect marriage, they certainly did not. He was vain and unfaithful, but he was loving too. And one of the ways he loved her most was through his encouragement. He believed in her. He believed that someday she would be true to her calling. Now, as she walked along the beach, the sand swarming around her legs, she believed too. She had done the caretaker thing for years, and especially in the last months before Trace's death. Now that he was gone, and the kids were gone, she was faced with a decision: find herself or lose herself.

When she lifted her eyes from the beach where she had been staring as she walked, she suddenly saw the most magical sight. Ponies. Everywhere it seemed there were ponies. Fat brown ponies with shaggy winter coats and ponies whose coats looked like slabs of marble. Golden ponies with long white manes that blew in the wind. Strawberry roans and bays. The sight of them, galloping in a swift ribbon on the beach, took Vera's breath away. *That's why I came this way*, she thought to herself and the next thing she knew, she had fallen in a deep hole. The lid of the urn had come off and Trace's ashes were being whipped up by the wind and carried off to sea.

"No!" Vera cried, struggling to get up and chase the urn down. When she finally did reach it, there was little of Trace left inside. Vera stood at the water's edge, her boots soaked and her spirits demolished, and cried.

"Need some help?" a husky voice asked her. It was the fisherman with the pole and his empty bucket. Without lifting her head, Vera just shook her head no. "Well, let me at least get you out of this water. The tide's rising," he said, taking her lightly by the arm. "Mighty cold to be at the beach now. This time of year, we're likely to get a storm."

She rose, with his help, and stood face to face with the husky-voiced man, who was so much taller than she, and lanky. There was something vaguely familiar about him, about what he said. She couldn't place it, but as soon as those words came out of his mouth, she knew. She knew what she was doing here. What Trace would have wanted for her? To write up a storm.

"Thank you for stopping," she said, "but I'm really fine. Just an accident. Serendipity really. It's been a pleasure meeting you!" she called as she walked briskly down the beach away from him, clutching the urn with what little remained of her dead husband. Enough to scatter under the rose bushes. To nurture peace.

"But we haven't met! My name is Chris Mann!" he yelled after her. "Where are you staying?" Vera just waved her hand over her head and kept walking. The writer in Vera knew that there were several ways this could go. One: she could tell him where she was staying and he could break in during the night and rape her, rob her, or leave her there to die. Since that seemed improbable, Vera came up with scenario two: they could exchange numbers, chat, get to know each other and fall in love. Too soon, she told herself and created option three: I walk away, anonymous, and take care of my own life for once, without interruption. Vera smiled at the sound of that. *No man*, she thought to herself, *is going to keep me from my goal now.*

Back at the cottage, appropriately named *Precious Gems* (how had she missed that sign before?), Vera settled herself into the study with a cup of hot tea. She sat at the desk in the comfy leather chair and wondered how many other writers had sat here, new writers like herself who had never written a novel before. For a moment, panic seized her. Who was she kidding? She didn't know the first thing about writing books. But then, she heard a voice tell her, "Go on. What else have you got to do? If it's awful, rip it up. But you'll never get anywhere if you don't try." She smoothed the pages of her journal back and played with the lid of her precision marker.

"Go on," she heard her sister Ronnie say as Vera stood, at 8 years old, on the edge of the quarry in her little orange bathing suit. "Don't be a coward. Just jump." Despite a fear so intense it set her knees knocking, she had jumped, almost certain that she was going to die. She leapt then because she was afraid not to leap, afraid of the ridicule and jokes. She jumped because she didn't know how not to jump. She really had no choice. But once she had taken the leap out into the air and into the cold, cold water below, she felt an elation that she had never known before. And she ran back to do it again.

At that minute, so many years later, Vera knew what she had to do. She wasn't afraid as much as breathless at the opportunity to once again leap into the unknown and see what emerged. She believed that whatever came of this exercise, it would be for the good. Trace had set her free and God had given her the greatest gift anyone can ask for. It wasn't faith, though she had faith in the Universe that she was on the right path. Hope? Of course, she had hope that her dreams would be fulfilled.

Picking up the little frame with the poem in it, she read again. *We play at paste/til qualified for pearl.* Suddenly, a memory came back to her of when she had first heard that poem, forty years before. She was on a bus, going into Boston, and a man had sat down beside her and reached into his pocket. Out came a little book of poetry by Emily Dickinson. He read silently and smiled to himself, then came to a stop and looked at her. She was in her late teens, and she was lost. Her life had no meaning, so she drank and smoked pot and slept around hoping to give herself some purpose. The little man in his Burberry trench coat asked if he could read her *Gem-tactics* and she, apathetically, agreed to listen. The poem was lost on her but she knew it meant something. Something, he told her, that someday she would understand if she only kept going long enough. Long enough had arrived. She'd practiced long enough. It was time to write, and she'd start with what she knew. *Iowa was hot and flat in 1963.*

EPILOGUE

ONE SUMMER DAY, VERA, NOW IN HER 70S, STOOD AT THE SINK IN the kitchen of the farmhouse in Vermont that she had moved into to celebrate the beginning of a new life. The turmoil of the last decade was over, and every morning she looked out her kitchen window onto the bowl of mountains and a telling sky. Today, the resplendent blue heralded a lovely day, and as she watched her granddaughters —Lucy, 8, and Olive, 5—blow magnificent bubbles and chase them, giggling and shrieking, she knew that for that moment everything was all right.

Lucy and Olive, Rose's little toe-headed waifs, had come to spend the week with Vera while Rose attended some yoga course in New Mexico, to help her practice. The girls had kept Vera busy, with walks around the lake and up the mountain, horseback riding and blueberry picking that left Vera breathless and tired at night, so tired she fell asleep when her head hit the pillow. But she wasn't complaining. She loved being with them, listening to them, and watching them. Now, the little girls appeared in the kitchen, panting.

"Grandma!" they cried, "Can we have a lemonade stand?"

QUESTIONS FOR DISCUSSION

1. Whose story is this? One interpretation might say it is Vera's story, given that it is through her eyes that we are seeing the characters unfold. Is that just scratching the surface? Could there be a broader message, one that entails seeing the sisters as more than just siblings, but rather representatives of all women growing up at that time?

2. How do the historical events described in the novel directly and indirectly shape the lives of the Book family? In what way does history repeat itself, come full circle, in the book?

3. Why did Valley allow Vera to have a lemonade stand? How was this request ironic in terms of the setting and yet characteristic of Valley early in the book? In what ways is *The Book Sisters* an optimistic novel?

4. Madison Smartt Bell calls *The Book Sisters* a "dark comedy." Where do you see hope rising from the ashes in the novel? How is the juxtaposition of the negative with the positive necessary to convey the overall message? When have you found yourself teetering between sorrow and joy, pain and pleasure? What insights followed?

5. What did you notice about the author's use of description in establishing the settings in the novel? When Victoria and Mama Poole notice the first snowdrops, when Vera and Violet breathe

in the pine air, do the details flesh out the scene, contribute to characterization, or do they distract from the narrative?

6. Compare how Vera's family saw her to how others saw her, to how she saw herself. How did Vera try to fill the "hole in her soul"? To what did her parents and sisters turn to mask their own suffering? Have you ever found yourself turning to substances or activities to mask your pain? Did it work?

7. When Valley and Vern died, the girls are described, in the chapter titled *Buzz*, in metaphors and images – a locomotive, a thousand balloons rising, etc. Which of these images worked the best for you and why? In what ways are they harbingers of things to come?

8. Why do you suppose the author chose Vera as the narrator of the book? How different would the story have been if Virginia, or Victoria, had told it? Did the author make the right choice?

9. Once Valley and Vern are gone, the sisters are free to write their own futures. But are they really free? Do they grow and change due to their parents' deaths, or do they stay static in the roles that they have assumed, based on what their options have been thus far? In what way does society shape their lives?

10. The author chose to tell the story in vignettes, short bursts of memories in the life of the family. Would you have felt more satisfied if this had been a "regular" novel? Do you feel that the way the story was told allowed you enough, or too little, access to become emotionally involved with the characters?

11. At the end of the novel, Vera comes across a poem by Emily Dickinson titled "Gem Tactics." The gist of the poem is that we start out in life pretending who we are, but gradually, through time and change, we become the real thing. Is Vera's

transformation complete and believable? How do you know that she is finally, truly, okay with who she is? Was this a satisfying ending to the book for you?